THE COLLECTED WORKS OF S. MUKERJI:

INDIAN GHOST STORIES

AND

THE MYSTERIOUS TRADERS

Uncredited woodcut print from region of Calcutta, India; late 19th Century.

THE COLLECTED WORKS OF S. MUKERJI:

Indian Ghost Stories

and

The Mysterious Traders

Edited by

Eric J. Guignard

DARK MOON BOOKS
Los Angeles, California

The Collected Works of S. Mukerji:
Indian Ghost Stories and The Mysterious Traders

Edited by Eric J. Guignard

Text from *Indian Ghost Stories* is that of the fourth edition,
published by A.H. Wheeler & Co. (Allahabad, India), 1921.

Text from *The Mysterious Traders* is that of the first publication,
serialized in *East & West* journal (Bombay, India), Oct.–Dec., 1913.

Introduction © 2024 by K. Hari Kumar
www.wikipedia.org/wiki/K._Hari_Kumar

Annotations and all other supplemental material © 2024 by Eric J. Guignard

Interior layout by Eric J. Guignard
Cover design by Eric J. Guignard
www.ericjguignard.com

Cover art by Warwick Goble: interior illustration from
Folk-Tales of Bengal (by Lal Behari Day), 1912 edition.

First edition published in November, 2024

Library of Congress Cataloging-in-Publication Data
The collected works of S. Mukerji: Indian ghost stories and the mysterious traders /
edited by Eric J. Guignard.

Library of Congress Control Number: 2024942464

ISBN-13: 978-1-949491-59-3 (hardback)
ISBN-13: 978-1-949491-57-9 (paperback)
ISBN-13: 978-1-949491-58-6 (e-book)

DARK MOON BOOKS
Los Angeles, California
www.DarkMoonBooks.com

Made in the United States of America
DMB 10 9 8 7 6 5 4 3 2 1

(V101624)

Dedicated to the ghosts
and ghost makers
around the world.

And to
Lisa Morton and Leslie S. Kilinger
for inspiring an appreciation
of annotations.

Mid-1920s railway guide (timetable) for the Assam-Bengal (northeast India) line, which ran 1892–1942. Railway station bookstalls were a principal source of sales for S. Mukerji's works.

CONTENTS

Illustration by Ernest Griset from *Vikram and the Vampire, or Tales of Hindu Devilry* by Richard F. Burton, F.R.G.S. (1870).

FOREWORD

BY K. HARI KUMAR

I GREW up steeped in stories of the supernatural, passed down through the generations by my grandmothers. Their folktales, told in hushed, reverent tones, were populated by spectral figures—*yakshis*, *dakinis*, *rakshasas*, *bhootas*, and *pretas*—beings that, in the deep south of Kerala, were as real as the land itself. These chilling stories, drawn from the ancient well of southern India's folklore, were constant reminders of the invisible world that coexisted with our own. Yet, as a boy growing up in Delhi, far from the verdant landscapes of my ancestral home, I encountered an entirely different realm of spirits. My landlady, a woman of Punjabi heritage, often shared tales of her own region—stories of *churels* or enchantresses with inverted feet and goblins that stole souls, a haunted world shaped by the spectral echoes of pre-Partition Punjab.

Later, in my teenage years, as I delved into American and English horror, I found a striking contrast to the ghostly tales I had grown up with. Yet, it was the stories from Bengal, shared by my Bengali friends in a new neighborhood in Gurugram, that left the most lasting impression. Fittingly, S. Mukerji is a Bengali name, and many of the accounts in this collection originate from that very region. Bengal, home to the erstwhile British capital of Calcutta, absorbed the Gothic sensibilities of its colonial past and intertwined them with its rich local lore. In this cultural crucible, the Victorian British ghost story met the timeless Bengali *bhoot*, producing an atmospheric magic that was both haunting and magnetic. It was then, as it is now, that I understood Indian ghost stories to be far more than regional curiosities; they are profound expressions deeply rooted in our collective cultural psyche, woven into the very fabric of the nation's identity.

There is a profound commonality that runs through the horror traditions of this vast and diverse nation—a shared thread that binds the land and its people to the supernatural. At the heart of this lies the belief in *punarjanma*, the cycle of rebirth, a concept that shapes much of Indian religion and spirituality. The *aatman*, the immortal soul, does not perish with the body; instead, it moves from one life to the next, caught in an eternal journey. But when a soul clings too tightly to the world it has left behind—unable to release its attachments—it becomes a restless presence, a wandering spirit trapped between realms. And such entities become central subjects of our folklore.

What makes Indian ghost stories particularly unique is that not all spectral beings are malevolent. Some are lost souls, lingering helplessly between worlds, while others are venerated—spirits that, if appeased, can offer protection or even blessings. In certain cases, they are seen as attendants of Shiva, the destroyer god, whose association with both creation and destruction reflects the dual nature of these entities. In India, ghosts are not fleeting apparitions but are woven into a much larger cosmic order, shaped by the spiritual frameworks of Hinduism, Buddhism, and other traditions that have flourished across the subcontinent. Whether it is the forlorn *bhoot*, the alluring yet deadly *churel*, or the vengeful *preta*, these beings are deeply connected to the rituals, beliefs, and unresolved tasks of their past lives. They inhabit the world as fully as the living, embodying the profound interconnection between life, death, and rebirth that defines Indian spirituality.

This collection, though featuring stories from northern and eastern India, resonates with something far deeper than mere ghostly encounters. However, to call them mere stories would not be accurate, as it is more a series of accounts of real hauntings and strange phenomena. In one story in particular, "The Messenger of Death", Mukerji masterfully intertwines these accounts with an acute understanding of how deeply superstition and the supernatural are connected to the land, leaving the reader with an unsettling sense of the uncanny. Another piece, "The Boy Possessed", explores incidents where the dead manifest through the bodies of the living to express grievances about the neglected state of their resting places.

It is this unique perspective on death—and what lies beyond—that imbues Indian ghost stories with their true power. These are not simply tales designed to terrify; they reflect a belief system that views death not as an end, but as a transition, where the boundaries between the living and the dead remain fluid and ever shifting. In this physical realm we call reality, spirits—like memories—never truly fade. They linger, suspended in time, their presence as tangible and enduring as the stories that keep them alive.

As Eric J. Guignard has debated elsewhere in this book, the true identity of S. Mukerji may remain shrouded in mystery, but these stories transport me back to an era overshadowed by the British Raj, when the land itself seemed to resonate with echoes of another world, all while grappling with its own internal battles for identity and survival. What stands out most in

Mukerji's work is his deft exploration of uniquely Indian cultural concepts, from a European perspective at best, which he renders accessible without losing the intrinsic depth. Take, for instance, the story "The Bridal Party", where the concept of *kanyadaan*—a tradition that might initially seem unfamiliar to Western readers—is skillfully unpacked. Mukerji presents it with a sensitivity that preserves its cultural essence while making it understandable. And where additional context is needed, Eric has done an admirable job of providing it, ensuring that even readers with no connection to the subcontinent can fully engage with and appreciate these stories.

Eric's dedication in curating this collection is praiseworthy, as he preserves not only the eerie essence of these tales but also opens a door for readers unfamiliar with India's lores and "horror" landscape. However, I must be honest—while these stories offer a tantalizing glimpse into Indian supernatural lore, they merely scratch the surface of what constitutes *true* Indian horror. For those brave enough to explore further, there is a vast, hidden world waiting to be uncovered.

K. Hari Kumar
September 17, 2024
Pune, India

K. HARI KUMAR is a bestselling Indian author, screenwriter, and filmmaker, celebrated for his expertise in Indian horror and mythology. With a career spanning across literature and film, he has become one of India's most recognized names in English-language horror. His works, deeply rooted in Indian folklore, occult traditions, and regional mythology, have captivated readers and audiences alike. Kumar has written eight books, including *India's Most Haunted*, *Daiva*, and *Dakini*, all published by HarperCollins. His anthology *India's Most Haunted* is considered one of the most popular horror story collections in India, and has been translated into multiple regional languages.

Kumar's versatility extends to cinema, where he has contributed as a screenwriter and filmmaker, with works such as the acclaimed web series *Bhram*. He frequently speaks at literary festivals and appears on popular podcasts to share his insights into the supernatural and otherworldly.

INDIAN
GHOST STORIES

S. MUKERJI

FOURTH EDITION.

ALLAHABAD:

A. H. WHEELER & CO.

1921.

Original title page of *Indian Ghost Stories* (fourth edition), 1921.

Printed by
A.H. Wheeler & Co.[*]
Allahabad.[†]

---

[*] Famous Indian-owned bookstore chain that once had a monopoly on Indian railway station bookstalls. (Notable also for publishing work by Rudyard Kipling.)
[†] Now Prayagraj; Allahabad was formerly the capital of the North-Western Provinces of India.

Interior illustration by W. (Warwick) Goble
from *Folk-tales of Bengal* (1912).
Herein, a benevolent Brahmadaitya saves a Brahmin
woodcutter from a group of *Bhoot* (ghosts).

PREFACE TO THE
FIRST EDITION

I DO not know whether writing ghost stories is a mistake.

Most readers will like a ghost story in which towards the end it is found that the ghost was really a cat or a dog or a mischievous boy.

Such ghost stories are a source of pleasure, and are read as a pastime and are often vastly enjoyed, because though the reader is a bit afraid of what he does not know, still he likes to be assured that ghosts do not in reality exist.

Such ghost stories I have often myself read and enjoyed. The last one I read was in the December (1913) number of the *English Illustrated Magazine*. In that story coincidence follows coincidence in such beautiful succession that a young lady really believes that she sees a ghost and even feels its touch, and finally it turns out that it is only a monkey.

This is bathos that unfortunately goes too far. Still, I am sure, English readers love a ghost story of this kind.

It, however, cannot be denied that particular incidents do sometimes happen in such a way that they take our breath away. Here is something to the point.

"Twenty years ago, near Honey Grove, in Texas, James Ziegland, a wealthy young farmer won the hand of Metilda Tichnor, but jilted her a few days before the day fixed for the marriage. The girl, a celebrated beauty, became despondent and killed herself. Her brother, Phil, went to James Ziegland's home and after denouncing him, fired at him. The bullet grazed the cheek of the faithless lover and buried itself in a tree. Young Tichnor, supposing he had killed the man, put a bullet into his own head, dying instantly. Ziegland, subsequently married a wealthy widow. All this was, of course 20 years ago. The other day the farmer James Ziegland and his son cut down the tree in which Tichnor's bullet had lodged. The tree proved too tough for splitting and so a small charge of dynamite was used. The explosion discharged the long forgotten bullet with great force, it pierced Ziegland's head and he fell mortally wounded. He explained the existence of the mysterious bullet as he lay on his deathbed."—*The Pioneer, Allahabad*, (India,) 31st January, 1913.

In India, ghosts and their stories are looked upon with respect and fear. I have heard all sorts of ghost stories from my nurse and my father's coachman, Abdullah, who used to be my constant companion in my childhood (dear friend, who is no more), as well as from my friends who are Judges and Magistrates and other responsible servants of Government, and in two cases from Judges of Indian High Courts.

A story told by a nurse or a coachman should not certainly be reproduced in this book. In this book, there are a few of those stories only which are true to the best of the author's knowledge and belief.

Some of these narratives may, no doubt, savour too much of the nature of a Cock and Bull story[*], but the reader must remember that "there are more things in heaven and earth[†], etc." and that truth is sometimes stranger than fiction.

The author is responsible for the arrangement of the stories in this volume. Probably they could have been better arranged; but a little thought will make it clear why this particular sequence has been selected.

S.M.

CALCUTTA[‡],
July 1914.

---

[*] A story that is ridiculous and implausible.
[†] From William Shakespeare's *Hamlet* (Act 1, Scene 5): "There are more things in Heaven and Earth, Horatio, than are dreamt of in your philosophy."
[‡] Now Kolkata.

PREFACE TO THE SECOND EDITION

SINCE the publication of the first edition my attention has been drawn to a number of very interesting and instructive articles that have been appearing in the papers from time to time. Readers, who care for subjects like the present, must have themselves noted these. There is, however, one article "the *Occult Review* of January 1917" which, by reason of the great interest created in the German Kaiser at the present moment, I am forced to reproduce. But as permission to do so was delayed, the book was through the press by the time it arrived. I am therefore reproducing that article here. My grateful thanks are due to the proprietors and the Editor of "the *Occult Review*," but for whose kind permission some of my readers would have been deprived of a most interesting treat.

S.M.

ALLAHABAD,
July 18, 1917.

WILHELM II AND THE WHITE LADY
OF THE HOHENZOLLERNS.

BY KATHARINE COX.[*]

A great deal has been written and said concerning the various appearances of the famous White Lady of the Hohenzollerns. As long ago as the fifteenth century she was seen, for the first time, in the old Castle of Neuhaus, in Bohemia, looking out at noon day from an upper window of an uninhabited turret of the castle, and numerous indeed are the stories of her

---

[*] [Author's note:] The writer desires to acknowledge her indebtedness for much of the information contained in this article to J.H. Lavaur's "La Dame Blanche des Hohenzollern et Guillaume II" (Paris: 56 Rue d'Aboukir).

appearances to various persons connected with the Royal House of Prussia, from that first one in the turret window down to the time of the death of the late Empress Augusta, which was, of course, of comparatively recent date.[*] For some time after that event, she seems to have taken a rest; and now, if rumour is to be credited, the apparition which displayed in the past so deep an interest in the fortunes—or perhaps one would be more correct in saying misfortunes—of the Hohenzollern family has been manifesting herself again!

The remarkable occurrences of which I am about to write were related by certain French persons of sound sense and unimpeachable veracity, who happened to be in Berlin a few weeks before the outbreak of the European War. The Kaiser, the most superstitious monarch who ever sat upon the Prussian throne, sternly forbade the circulation of the report of these happenings in his own country, but our gallant Allies across the Channel are, fortunately, not obliged to obey the despotic commands of Wilhelm II, and these persons, therefore, upon their return to France, related, to those interested in such matters, the following story of the great War Lord's three visitations from the dreaded ghost of the Hohenzollerns.

Early in the summer of 1914 it was rumoured, in Berlin, that the White Lady had made her re-appearance. The tale, whispered first of all at Court, spread, gradually amongst the townspeople. The Court, alarmed, tried to suppress it, but it refused to be suppressed, and eventually there was scarcely a man, woman or child in the neighbourhood who did not say—irrespective of whether they believed it or not—that the White Lady, the shadowy spectre whose appearance always foreboded disaster to the Imperial House, had been recently seen, not once, but three times, and by no less a person than Kaiser Wilhelm himself!

The first of these appearances, so rumour stated, took place one night at the end of June. The hour was late: the Court, which was then in residence at the palace of Potsdam, was wrapped in slumber; all was quiet. There was an almost death-like silence in the palace. In one wing were the apartments of the Empress, where she lay sleeping; in the opposite wing slept one of her sons; the other Princes were in Berlin. In an entirely different part of the royal residence, guarded by three sentinels in a spacious antechamber,

---

[*] There are many suggested origins for "White Lady" lore found throughout Germany; the White Lady of the Hohenzollerns is alternately claimed to be the spirit of Princess Bertha Von Rosenberg, mistress Anna Sydow, or Countess Kunlzunde of Orlamunde, among others.

sat the Emperor in his private study. He had been lately, greatly engrossed in weighty matters of State, and for some time past it had been his habit to work thus, far into the night. That same evening the Chancellor, von Bethman-Hollweg, had had a private audience of his Majesty, and had left the royal presence precisely at 11.30, carrying an enormous *dossier* under his arm. The Emperor had accompanied him as far as the door, shaken hands with him, then returned to his work at his writing-desk.

Midnight struck, and still the Emperor, without making the slightest sound, sat on within the room. The guards without began to grow slightly uneasy, for at midnight punctually—not a minute before, not a minute after—it was the Emperor's unfailing custom, when he was working late at night, to ring and order a light repast to be brought to him. Sometimes it used to be a cup of thick chocolate, with hot cakes; sometimes a few sandwiches of smoked ham with a glass of Munich or Pilsen beer—but, as this particular midnight hour struck the guards awaited the royal commands in vain. The Emperor had apparently forgotten to order his midnight meal!

One o'clock in the morning came, and still the Emperor's bell had not sounded. Within the study silence continued to reign—silence as profound indeed as that of the grave. The uneasiness of the three guards without increased; they glanced at each other with anxious faces. Was their royal master taken ill? All during the day he had seemed to be labouring under the influence of some strange, suppressed excitement, and as he had bidden good-bye to the Chancellor they had noticed that the expression of excitement on his face had increased. That something of grave import was in the air they, and indeed every one surrounding the Emperor, had long been aware, it was just possible that the strain of State affairs was becoming too much for him, and that he had been smitten with sudden indisposition. And yet, after all, he had probably only fallen asleep! Whichever it was, however, they were uncertain how to act. If they thrust ceremony aside and entered the study, they knew that very likely they would only expose themselves to the royal anger. The order was strict, "When the Emperor works in his study no one may enter it without being bidden." Should they inform the Lord Chamberlain of the palace? But, if there was no sufficiently serious reason for such a step, they would incur *his* anger, almost as terrible to face as that of their royal master.

A little more time dragged by, and at last, deciding to risk the consequences, the guards approached the study. One of them, the most courageous of the three, lifted a heavy curtain, and slowly and cautiously opened the door. He gave one rapid glance into the room beyond, then, returning to his companions said in a low voice and with a terrified gesture towards the interior of the study:

"Look!"

The two guards obeyed him, and an alarming spectacle met their eyes. In the middle of the room, beside a big table littered with papers and military documents, lay the Emperor, stretched full length upon the thick velvet pile carpet, one hand, as if to hide something dreadful from view, across his face. He was quite unconscious, and while two of the guards endeavoured to revive him, the other ran for the doctor. Upon the doctor's arrival they carried him to his sleeping apartments, and after some time succeeded in reviving him. The Emperor then, in trembling accents, told his astounded listeners what had occurred.

Exactly at midnight, according to his custom, he had rung the bell which was the signal that he was ready for his repast. Curiously enough, neither of the guards, although they had been listening for it, had heard that bell.

He had rung quite mechanically, and also mechanically, had turned again to his writing desk directly he had done so. A few minutes later he had heard the door open and footsteps approach him across the soft carpet. Without raising his head from his work he had commenced to say:

"Bring me—"

Then he had raised his head, expecting to see the butler awaiting his orders. Instead his eyes fell upon a shadowy female figure dressed in white, with a long, flowing black veil trailing behind her on the ground. He rose from his chair, terrified, and cried:

"Who are you, and what do you want?"

At the same moment, instinctively, he placed his hand upon a service revolver which lay upon the desk. The white figure, however, did not move, and he advanced towards her. She gazed at him, retreating slowly backwards towards the end of the room, and finally disappeared through the door which gave access to the antechamber without. The door, however, had not opened, and the three guards stationed in the antechamber, as has been already stated, had neither seen nor heard anything of the apparition. At the moment of her disappearance the Emperor fell into a swoon, remaining in that condition until the guards and the doctor revived him.

Such was the story, gaining ground every day in Berlin, of the first of the three appearances of the White Lady of the Hohenzollerns to the Kaiser. The story of her second appearance to him, which occurred some two or three weeks later, is equally remarkable.

On this occasion she did not visit him at Potsdam, but at Berlin, and instead of the witching hour of midnight, she chose the broad, clear light of day. Indeed, during the whole of her career, the White Lady does not seem to have kept to the time-honoured traditions of most ghosts, and appeared to startled humanity chiefly at night time or in dim uncertain lights. She has never been afraid to face the honest daylight, and that, in my opinion, has always been a great factor in establishing her claim to genuineness. A ghost who is seen by sane people, in full daylight, cannot surely be a mere legendary myth!

It was an afternoon of bright summer—that fateful summer whose blue skies were so soon to be darkened by the sinister clouds of war! The Royal Standard, intimating to the worthy citizens of Berlin the presence of their Emperor, floated gaily over the Imperial residence in the gentle breeze. The Emperor, wrapped in heavy thought—there was much for the mighty War Lord to think about during those last pregnant days before plunging Europe into an agony of tears and blood!—was pacing, alone, up and down a long gallery within the palace.

His walk was agitated; there was a troubled frown upon his austere countenance. Every now and then he paused in his walk, and withdrew from his pocket a piece of paper, which he carefully read and re-read, and as he did so, angry, muttered words broke from him, and his hand flew instinctively to his sword hilt. Occasionally he raised his eyes to the walls on either side of him, upon which hung numerous portraits of his distinguished ancestors. He studied them gravely, from Frederick I, Burgrave of Nuremburg, to that other Frederick, his own father, and husband of the fair English princess against whose country he was so shortly going to wage the most horrible warfare that has ever been waged in the whole history of the world!

Suddenly, from the other end of the long portrait gallery he perceived coming towards him a shadowy female figure, dressed entirely in white, and carrying a large bunch of keys in her hand. She was not, this time, wearing the long flowing black veil in which she had appeared to him a few weeks previously, but the Emperor instantly recognized her, and the blood froze in his veins. He stood rooted to the ground, unable to advance or to retreat, paralysed with horror, the hair rising on his head, beads of perspiration standing on his brow.

The figure continued to advance in his direction, slowly, noiselessly, appearing rather to glide than to walk over the floor. There was an expression of the deepest sadness upon her countenance, and as she drew near to the stricken man watching her, she held out her arms towards him, as if to enfold him. The Emperor, his horror increasing, made a violent effort to move, but in vain. He seemed indeed paralysed; his limbs, his muscles, refused to obey him.

Then suddenly, just as the apparition came close up to him and he felt, as on the former occasion when he had been visited by her, that he was going to faint, she turned abruptly and moved away in the direction of a small side door. This she opened with her uncanny bunch of keys and without turning her head, disappeared.

At the exact moment of her disappearance the Emperor recovered his faculties. He was able to move, he was able to speak; his arms, legs, tongue, obeyed his autocratic will once more. He uttered a loud terrified cry, which resounded throughout the palace. Officers, chamberlains, guards, servants, came running to the gallery, white-faced, to see what had happened. They found their royal master in a state bordering on collapse. Yet, to the anxious questions which they put to him, he only replied incoherently and evasively; it was as if he knew something terrible, something dreadful, but did not wish to speak of it. Eventually he retired to his own apartments, but it was not until several hours had passed that he returned to his normal condition of mind.

The same doctor who had been summoned on the occasion of Wilhelm's former encounter with the White Lady was in attendance on him, and he looked extremely grave when informed that the Emperor had again experienced a mysterious shock. He shut himself up alone with his royal patient, forbidding any one else access to the private apartments. However, in spite of all precautions, the story of what had really occurred in the picture gallery eventually leaked out—it is said through a maid of honour, who heard it from the Empress.

The third appearance of the White Lady of the Hohenzollerns to the Kaiser did not take place at either of the palaces, but strangely enough, in a forest, though exactly where situated has not been satisfactorily verified.

In the middle of the month of July, 1914, while the war-clouds were darkening every hour, the Emperor's movements were very unsettled. He was constantly travelling from place to place, and one day—so it was afterwards said in Berlin—while on a hunting expedition, he suddenly encountered a phantom female figure, dressed in white, who, springing apparently from nowhere, stopped in front of his horse, and blew a shadowy horn, frightening the animal so much that its rider was nearly thrown to the ground. The phantom figure then disappeared, as mysteriously as it had come—but that it was the White Lady of the Hohenzollerns, come, perchance, to warn Wilhelm of some terrible future fate, there was little doubt in the minds of those who afterwards heard of the occurrence.

According to one version of the story of this third appearance, the phantom was also seen by two officers who were riding by the Emperor's side, but the general belief is that she manifested herself, as on the two former occasions, to Wilhelm alone.

There are many who will not believe in the story, no doubt, and there are also many who will. For my own part, I am inclined to think that, if the ghost of the Hohenzollerns was able to manifest herself so often on the eve of any tragedy befalling them in past, it would be strange indeed if she had not manifested herself on the eve of this greatest tragedy of all—the War!

Suggested as the White Lady of the Hohenzollerns; 19ᵗʰ century illustration by Émile Vernier from the opera *La Dame Blanche* (*The White Lady*).

Portrait of a Young Indian Woman, by Sir Henry Raeburn, 1815.

HIS DEAD WIFE'S PHOTOGRAPH.

THIS story created a sensation when it was first told. It appeared in the papers and many big Physicists and Natural Philosophers were, at least so they thought, able to explain the phenomenon. I shall narrate the event and also tell the reader what explanation was given, and let him draw his own conclusions.

This was what happened.

A friend of mine, a clerk in the same office as myself, was an amateur photographer; let us call him Jones.

Jones had a half plate Sanderson camera[*] with a Ross lens and a Thornton Picard[†] behind lens shutter, with pneumatic release. The plate in question was a Wrattens ordinary, developed with Ilford Pyro Soda developer prepared at home. All these particulars I give for the benefit of the more technical reader.

Mr. Smith, another clerk in our office, invited Mr. Jones to take a likeness of his wife and sister-in-law.

This sister-in-law was the wife of Mr. Smith's elder brother, who was also a Government servant, then on leave. The idea of the photograph was of the sister-in-law.

Jones was a keen photographer himself. He had photographed every body in the office including the peons[‡] and sweepers, and had even supplied every sitter of his with copies of his handiwork. So he most willingly consented, and anxiously waited for the Sunday on which the photograph was to be taken.

Early on Sunday morning, Jones went to the Smiths'. The arrangement of light in the verandah was such that a photograph could only be taken after midday; and so he stayed there to breakfast.

At about one in the afternoon all arrangements were complete and the two ladies, Mrs. Smiths, were made to sit in two cane chairs and after long and careful focusing, and moving the camera about for an hour, Jones was satisfied at last and an exposure was made. Mr. Jones was sure that the plate was all right; and so, a second plate was not exposed although in the usual course of things this should have been done.

---

[*] Type of flexible bellows camera.

[†] Misspelling of Thornton-Pickard, a British camera manufacturer.

[‡] Low-ranking worker such as an attendant or assistant; the term was not considered offensive during this period of time, as it is now in contemporary usage.

He wrapped up his things and went home promising to develop the plate the same night and bring a copy of the photograph the next day to the office.

The next day, which was a Monday, Jones came to the office very early, and I was the first person to meet him.

"Well, Mr. Photographer," I asked, "what success?"

"I got the picture all right," said Jones, unwrapping an unmounted picture and handing it over to me. "Most funny, don't you think so?"

"No, I don't . . . I think it is all right, at any rate I did not expect anything better from you . . . " I said.

"No," said Jones, "the funny thing is that only two ladies sat . . . "

"Quite right," I said. "The third stood in the middle."

"There was no third lady at all there . . . " said Jones.

"Then you imagined she was there, and there we find her . . . "

"I tell you, there were only two ladies there when I exposed," insisted Jones. He was looking awfully worried.

"Do you want me to believe that there were only two persons when the plate was exposed and three when it was developed?" I asked.

"That is exactly what has happened," said Jones.

"Then it must be the most wonderful developer you used, or was it that this was the second exposure given to the same plate?"

"The developer is the one which I have been using for the last three years, and the plate, the one I charged on Saturday night out of a new box that I had purchased only in the afternoon that day."

A number of other clerks had come up in the meantime, and were taking great interest in the picture and in Jones' assertion.

It is only right that a description of the picture be given here for the benefit of the reader. I wish I could reproduce the original picture too, but that for certain reasons is impossible.

When the plate was actually exposed there were only two ladies, both of whom were sitting in cane chairs. When the plate was developed it was found that there was in the picture a figure, that of a lady, standing in the middle. She wore a broad-edged *dhoti** (the reader should not forget that all the characters are Indians); only the upper half of her body was visible, the lower being hidden from view by the low backs of the cane chairs. She was evidently behind the chairs, and consequently slightly out of focus. Still everything was quite clear. Even her long necklace was visible through the

---

* Unstitched cloth wrapped around the legs (to resemble trousers) and sometimes torso.

little opening in the *dhoti* near the right shoulder. She was resting her hands on the backs of the chairs and the fingers were nearly totally out of focus, but a ring on the right ring-finger was clearly visible. She looked like a handsome young woman of twenty-two, short and thin. One of the earrings was also clearly discernible, although the face itself was slightly out of focus. One thing, and probably the funniest thing, that we overlooked then but observed afterwards, was that immediately behind the three ladies was a barred window. The two ladies, who were one on each side, covered up the bars to a certain height from the bottom with their bodies, but the lady in the middle was partly transparent because the bars of the window were very faintly distinguishable through her. This fact, however, as I have said already, we did not observe then. We only laughed at Jones and tried to assure him that he was either drunk or asleep. At this moment Smith of our office walked in, removing the trouser-clips from his legs.

Smith took the unmounted photograph, looked at it for a minute, turned red and blue and green and finally very pale. Of course, we asked him what the matter was and this was what he said:

"The third lady in the middle was my first wife, who has been dead these eight years. Before her death she asked me a number of times to have her photograph taken. She used to say that she had a presentiment that she might die early. I did not believe in her presentiment myself, but I did not object to the photograph. So one day I ordered a carriage and asked her to dress up. We intended to go to a good professional. She dressed up and the carriage was ready, but as we were going to start news reached us that her mother was dangerously ill. So we went to see her mother instead. The mother was very ill, and I had to leave her there. Immediately afterwards I was sent away on duty to another station and so could not bring her back. It was in fact after full three months and a half that I returned and then though her mother was all right, my wife was not. Within fifteen days of my return she died of puerperal fever* after child-birth and the child died too. Thus it happened that her photograph was never taken. When she dressed up for the last time on the day that she left my home she had the necklace and the earrings on, as you see her wearing in the photograph. My present wife has them now but she does not generally use them."

This was too big a pill for me to swallow. So I at once took French leave† from my office, bagged the photograph and rushed out on my bicycle. I went

---

* Postpartum infection; a type of bacterial infection.

† Departure without asking permission or informing anyone; i.e. "walking out."

to Mr. Smith's house and looked Mrs. Smith up. Of course, she was much astonished to see a third lady in the picture but could not guess who she was. This I had expected, as supposing Smith's story to be true, this lady had never seen her husband's first wife. The elder brother's wife, however, recognized the likeness at once and she virtually repeated the story which Smith had told us in the morning. She even brought out the necklace and the earrings for my inspection and conviction. They were the same as those in the photograph.

All the principal newspapers of that time got hold of the fact and within a week there was any number of applications for the ghostly photograph. But Mr. Jones refused to supply copies of it to anybody for various reasons, the principal being that Smith would not allow it. I am, however, the fortunate possessor of a copy which, for obvious reasons, I am not allowed to show to anybody. One copy of the picture was sent to America and another to England. I do not now remember exactly to whom. My own copy I showed to the Rev. Father——[*]M.A., D.SC., B.D., etc., and asked him to find out a scientific explanation of the phenomenon. The following explanation was given by the gentleman. (I am afraid I shall not be able to reproduce the learned Father's exact words, but this is what he meant or at least what I understood him to mean).

"The girl in question was dressed in this particular way on an occasion, say ten years ago. Her image was cast *on space*[†] and the reflection was projected from one luminous body (one planet) on another till it made a circuit of millions and millions of miles in space and then came back to earth at the exact moment when your friend, Mr. Jones, was going to make the exposure.

"Take for instance the case of a man who is taking the photograph of a mirage. He is photographing place X from place Y, when X and Y are, say, two hundred miles apart, and it may be that his camera is facing east while place X is actually towards the west of place Y."

At school I had read a little of Science and Chemistry and could make a dry analysis of a salt; but this was an item too abstruse for my limited comprehension.

The fact, however, remains and I believe it, that Smith's first wife did

---

[*] The double em-dash was often utilized as a quaint method in literature of obscuring someone's name or location to keep them anonymous, i.e. for their supposed protection (or privacy).

[†] Cosmically.

come back to this terrestrial globe of ours over eight years after her death to give a sitting for a photograph in a form which, though it did not affect the retina of our eye, did impress a sensitized plate;—in a form that did not affect the retina of the eye, I say, because Jones must have been looking at his sitters at the time when he was pressing the bulb of the pneumatic release of his time and instantaneous shutter.

The story is most wonderful but this is exactly what happened. Smith says this is the first time he has ever seen, or heard from, his dead wife. It is popularly believed in India that a dead wife gives a lot of trouble, if she ever revisits this earth, but this is, thank God, not the experience of my friend, Mr. Smith.

It is now over seven years since the event mentioned above happened; and the dead girl has never appeared again. I would very much like to have a photograph of the two ladies taken once more; but I have never ventured to approach Smith with the proposal. In fact, I learnt photography myself with a view to take the photograph of the two ladies, but as I have said, I have never been able to speak to Smith about my intention, and probably never shall. The £10, that I spent on my cheap photographic outfit may be a waste. But I have learnt an art which though rather costly for my limited means is nevertheless worth learning, being, closely allied to the Art "That can immortalize, the art that baffles time's tyrannic claim.*"

After the publication of the third edition a similar incident was reported last year in one of the leading Anglo-Indian Dailies under the facetious heading of "Doyle out-Doyled." It is to this effect:—

When shortly after death a photograph was taken of a deceased person at Burdwan in Bengal there appeared in the finished copy a group comprising the corpse in the middle and three or four predeceased relations of that person sitting round the dead body.

---

* From "On Receipt of My Mother's Picture" by English poet William Cowper (1731–1800).

Uncredited illustration from 1876 of a large colonial bungalow in India.

THE MAJOR'S LEASE.

A CURIOUS little story was told the other day in a Civil Court in British India.

A certain military officer, let us call him Major Brown, rented a house in one of the big Cantonment* stations where he had been recently transferred with his regiment.

This gentleman had just arrived from England with his wife. He was the son of a rich man at home and so he could afford to have a large house. This was the first time he had come out to India and was consequently rather unacquainted with the manners and customs of this country.

Major Brown took this house on a long lease and thought he had made a bargain. The house was large and stood in the centre of a very spacious compound. There was a garden which appeared to have been carefully laid out once, but as the house had no tenant for a long time the garden looked more like a wilderness. There were two very well kept lawn tennis courts and these had a great attraction for the Major, who was very keen on tennis. The stablings and out-houses were commodious and the Major, who was thinking of keeping a few polo ponies, found the whole thing very satisfactory. Over and above everything he found the landlord very obliging. He had heard on board the steamer on his way out that Indian landlords were the worst class of human beings one could come across on the face of this earth, but this particular landlord looked like an exception to the general rule.

He consented to make at his own expense all the alterations that the Major wanted him to do, and these alterations were carried out to Major and Mrs. Brown's entire satisfaction.

On his arrival in this station Major Brown had put up at a hotel and after some alterations had been made, he ordered the house to be furnished. This was done in three or four days and then he moved in.

Annexed is a rough sketch of the house in question. The house was a very large one and there was a number of rooms, but we have nothing to do with all of them. The spots marked "C" and "E" represent two of the doors.

Here is a rough plan, the original of which was probably in the Major's handwriting.

---

* Military quarters (i.e. for a permanent station), specific to British use in South Asia.

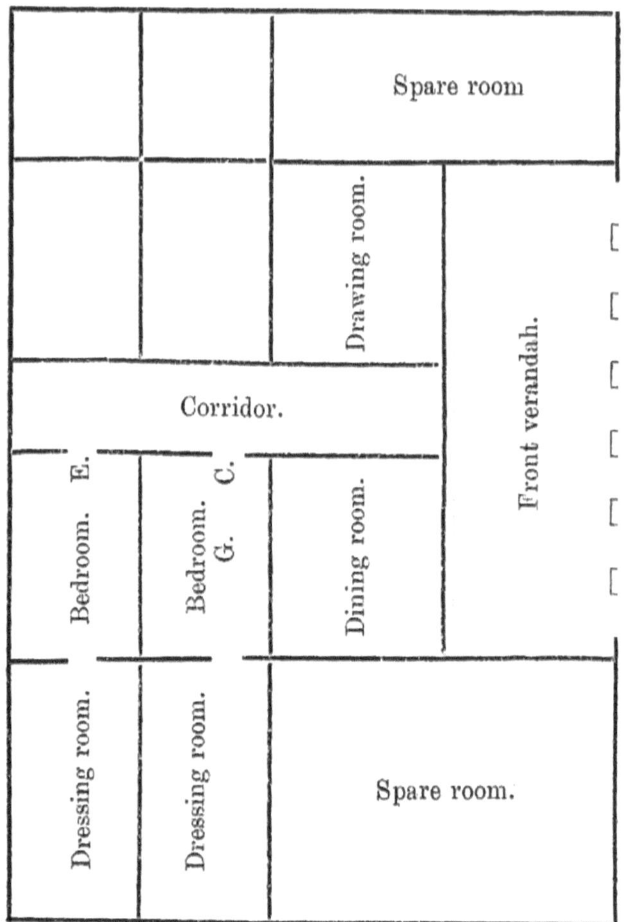

Original plan illustration for "The Major's Lease."

Now what happened in Court was this:

After he had occupied the house for not over three weeks the Major and his wife cleared out and took shelter again in the hotel from which they had come. The landlord demanded rent for the entire period stipulated for in the lease and the Major refused to pay. The matter went to Court. The presiding Judge, who was an Indian gentleman, was one of the cleverest men in the service, and he thought it was a very simple case.

When the case was called on, the plaintiff's pleader said that he would begin by proving the lease. Major Brown, the defendant, who appeared in person, said that he would admit it. The Judge who was a very kind hearted gentleman asked the defendant why he had vacated the house.

"I could not stay," said the Major. "I had every intention of living in the house, I got it furnished and spent two thousand rupees* over it, I was laying out a garden..."

"But what do you mean by saying that you could not stay?"

"If your Honour passed a night in that house, you would understand what I meant," said the Major.

"You take the oath and make a statement," said the Judge. Major Brown then made the following statement on oath in open Court.

"When I came to the station I saw the house and my wife liked it. We asked the landlord whether he would make a few alterations and he consented. After the alterations had been carried out I executed the lease and ordered the house to be furnished. A week after the execution of the lease we moved in. The house is very large."

Here followed a description of the building; but to make matters clear and short I have copied out the rough pencil sketch which is still on the record of the case and marked the doors and rooms, as in the original, with letters.

"I do not dine at the mess. I have an early dinner at home with my wife and retire early. My wife and I sleep in the same bedroom (the room marked "G" in the plan), and we are generally in bed at about eleven o'clock at night. The servants all go away to the out-houses which are at a distance of about forty yards from the main building, only one Jamadar (porter) remains in the front verandah. This Jamadar also keeps an eye on the whole main building, besides I have got a good, faithful watch dog which I brought out from home. He stays outside with the Jamadar.

"For the first fifteen days we were quite comfortable, then the trouble began.

"One night before dinner my wife was reading a story, a detective story, of a particularly interesting nature. There were only a few more pages left and so we thought that she would finish them before we put out the reading lamp. We were in the bedroom. But it took her much longer than she had expected it would, and so it was actually half an hour after midnight when we put out the big sixteen candle power reading lamp which stood on a teapoy† near the head of the beds. Only a small bedroom lamp remained.

"But though we put out the light we did not fall asleep. We were discussing the cleverness of the detective and the folly of the thief who had left a clue behind, and it was actually two o'clock when we pulled our rugs up to our necks and closed our eyes.

---

* Indian monetary unit (generally valued as small fraction of a British pound).
† Small wood table, similar to a nightstand or coffee table.

"At that moment we heard the footsteps of a number of persons walking along the corridor. The corridor runs the whole length of the house as will appear from the rough sketch. This corridor was well carpeted still we heard the tread of a number of feet. We looked at the door "C." This door was closed but not bolted from inside. Slowly it was pushed open, and, horror of horrors, three shadowy forms walked into the room. One was distinctly the form of a white man in European night attire, another the form of a white woman, also in night attire, and the third was the form of a black woman, probably an Indian nurse or ayah[*].

"We remained dumb with horror, as we could see clearly that these unwelcome visitors were not of this world. We could not move.

"The three figures passed right round the beds as if searching for something. They looked into every nook and corner of the bedroom and then passed into the dressing room. Within half a minute they returned and passed out into the corridor in the same order in which they had come in, namely, the man first, the white woman next, and the black woman last of all.

"We lay as if dead. We could hear them in the corridor and in the bedroom adjoining, with the door "E", and also in the dressing room attached to that bedroom. They again returned and passed into the ... and then we could hear them no more.

"It must have taken me at least five minutes to collect my senses and to bring my limbs under control. When I got up I found that my wife had fainted. I hurried out of the room, rushed along the corridor, opened the front door and called the servants. The servants were all approaching the house across the land which separated the servants' quarters from the main building, when I went into the dining room, and procuring some brandy, gave it to my wife. It was with some difficulty that I could make her swallow it, but it revived her and she looked at me with a bewildered smile on her face.

"The servants had in the meantime arrived and were in the corridor. Their presence had the effect of giving us some courage. Leaving my wife in bed I went out and related to the servants what I had seen. The *Chaukidar* (the night watchman) who was an old resident of the compound (in fact he had been in charge of the house when it was vacant, before I rented it) gave me the history of the ghosts, which my Jamadar interpreted to me. I have brought the *Chaukidar* and shall produce him as my witness."

This was the statement of the Major. Then there was the statement of Jokhi Passi, *Chaukidar*, defendant's witness.

The statement of this witness as recorded was as follows:

---

[*] Nanny.

"My age is sixty years. At the time of the Indian Mutiny I was a full-grown young man. This house was built at that time. I mean two or three years after the Mutiny. I have always been in charge. After the Mutiny one Judge came to live in the house. He was called Judge Parson (probably Pearson). The Judge had to try a young Muhammadan charged with murder and he sentenced the youth to death. The aged parents of the young man vowed vengeance against the good Judge. On the night following the morning on which the execution took place it appeared that certain undesirable characters were prowling about the compound. I was then the watchman in charge as I am now. I woke up the Indian nurse who slept with the Judge's baby in a bedroom adjoining the one in which the Judge himself slept. On waking up she found that the baby was not in its cot. She rushed out of the bedroom and informed the Judge and his wife. Then a feverish search began for the baby, but it was never found. The police were communicated with and they arrived at about four in the morning. The police enquiry lasted for about half an hour and then the officers went away promising to come again. At last the Judge, his wife, and nurse all retired to their respective beds where they were found lying dead later in the morning. Another police enquiry took place, and it was found that death was due to snake-bite. There were two small punctures on one of the legs of each victim. How a snake got in and killed each victim in turn, especially when two slept in one room and the third in another, and finally got out, has remained a mystery. But the Judge, his wife, and the nurse are still seen on every Friday night looking for the missing baby. One rainy season the servants' quarters were being re-roofed. I had then an occasion to sleep in the corridor; and thus I saw the ghosts. At that time I was as afraid as the Major Saheb* is to-day, but then I soon found out that the ghosts were quite harmless."

This was the story as recorded in Court. The Judge was a very sensible man (I had the pleasure and honour of being introduced to him about twenty years after this incident), and with a number of people, he decided to pass one Friday night in the haunted house. He did so. What he saw does not appear from the record: for he left no inspection notes and probably he never made any. He delivered judgment on Monday following. It is a very short judgment.

After reciting the facts the judgment proceeds: "I have recorded the statements of the defendant and a witness produced by him. I have also made a local inspection. I find that the landlord (the plaintiff) knew that for certain reasons the house was practically uninhabitable, and he concealed that fact from his tenant. He, therefore, could not recover. The suit is dismissed with costs."

---

* Also as "Sahib." Polite title or form of address for a man (e.g. "Doctor Sahib").

The haunted house remained untenanted for a long time. The proprietor subsequently made a gift of it to a charitable institution. The founders of this institution, who were Hindus and firm believers in charms and exorcisms, had some religious ceremony performed on the premises. Afterwards the house was pulled down and on its site now stands one of the grandest buildings in the station, that cost fully £10,000. Only this morning I received a visit from a gentleman who lives in the building, referred to above, but evidently he has not even heard of the ghosts of the Judge, his wife, and his Indian ayah.

It is now nearly fifty years; but the missing baby has not been heard of. If it is alive it has grown into a fully developed man. But does he know the fate of his parents and his nurse?

In this connection it will not be out of place to mention a fact that appeared in the papers some years ago.

A certain European gentleman was posted to a district in the Madras Presidency as a Government servant in the Financial Department.

This gentleman on reaching the station to which he had been posted put up at the Club, as they usually do, and began to look out for a house, when he was informed that there was a haunted house in the neighbourhood. Being rather sceptical he decided to take this house, ghost or no ghost. He was given to understand by the members of the Club that this house was a bit out of the way and was infested at night with thieves and robbers who came to divide their booty in that house; and to guard against its being occupied by a tenant it had been given a bad reputation. The proprietor being a wealthy old native of the old school did not care to investigate. So our friend, whom we shall, for the purposes of this story, call Mr. Hunter, took the house at a fair rent.

The house was in charge of a *Chaukidar* (care-taker, porter or watchman) when it was vacant. Mr. Hunter engaged that person as a night watchman for this house. This *Chaukidar* informed Mr. Hunter that the ghost appeared only one day in the year, namely, the twenty-first of September and added that if Mr. Hunter kept out of the house on that night there would be no trouble.

"I always keep away on the night of the twenty-first September," said the watchman.

"And what kind of ghost is it?" asked Mr. Hunter.

"It is a European lady dressed in white," said the man.

"What does she do?" inquired Mr. Hunter.

"Oh! she comes out of the room and calls you and asks you to follow her," said the man.

"Has anybody ever followed her?"

"Nobody that I know of, Sir," replied the *Chaukidar*. "The man who was here before me saw her and died from fear."

"Rather strange! But why do not people follow her in a body?" asked Mr. Hunter.

"It is very easy to say that, Sir, but when you see her you will not like to follow her yourself. I have been in this house for over twenty years; lots of times European soldiers have passed the night of the twenty-first September, intending to follow her, but when she actually comes nobody has ever ventured."

"Most wonderful!" remarked Mr. Hunter. "I shall follow her this time."

"As you please, Sir," said the man and retired.

It was one of the duties of Mr. Hunter to distribute the pensions of all retired Government servants. In this connection Mr. Hunter used to come into contact with a number of old men in the station who attended his office to receive their pensions from him. By questioning them Mr. Hunter got thus far that the house had at one time been occupied by a European officer.

This officer had a young wife who fell in love with a certain Captain Leslie. One night when the husband was out on tour (and not expected to return within a week) his wife was entertaining Captain Leslie. The gentleman returned unexpectedly and found his wife in the arms of the Captain.

He lost his self-control and attacked the couple with a meat chopper—the first weapon that came handy.

The craven-hearted captain decamped hastily leaving the unfortunate wife to the mercy of the infuriated husband. He aimed a blow at her head which she warded off with her hand. But so severe was the blow that the hand was cut off and the woman fell down on the ground quite unconscious. The sight of blood made the husband mad. Subsequently the servants came up and called in a doctor, but by the time the doctor arrived the woman was dead.

The unfortunate husband who had become raving mad was sent to a lunatic asylum and thence taken away to England. The body of the woman was in the local cemetery; but what had become of the severed hand was not known. The missing limb had never been found. All this was fifty years ago, that is, immediately after the Indian Mutiny.

This was what Mr. Hunter further gathered by dint of cross examination.

The twenty-first of September was not very far off. Mr. Hunter decided to meet the ghost.

The night in question arrived, and Mr. Hunter sat in his bedroom with his magazine. The lamp was burning brightly.

The servants had all retired, and Mr. Hunter knew that if he called for help nobody would hear him, and even if anybody did hear, he too would not come.

He was, however, a very bold man and sat there awaiting developments.

At one in the morning he heard footsteps approaching the bedroom from the direction of the dining-room.

He could distinctly hear the rustle of the skirts. Gradually the door between the two rooms began to open wide slowly. Then the curtain began to move. Mr. Hunter sat with straining eyes and beating heart.

At last she came in. The Englishwoman in flowing white robes. Mr. Hunter sat panting unable to move. She looked at him for about a minute and beckoned him to follow her. It was then that Mr. Hunter observed that she had only one hand.

He got up and followed her. She went back to the dining-room and he followed her there. There was no light in the dining-room but he could see her faintly in the dark. She went right across the dining-room to the door on the other side which opened on the verandah. Mr. Hunter could not see what she was doing at the door, but he knew she was opening it.

When the door opened she passed out and Mr. Hunter followed. Then she walked across the verandah down the steps and stood upon the lawn. Mr. Hunter was on the lawn in a moment. His fears had now completely vanished. She next proceeded along the lawn in the direction of a hedge. Mr. Hunter also reached the hedge and found that under the hedge were concealed two spades. The gardener must have been working with them and left them there after the day's work.

The lady made a sign to him and he took up one of the spades. Then again she proceeded and he followed.

They had reached some distance in the garden when the lady with her foot indicated a spot and Mr. Hunter inferred that she wanted him to dig there. Of course, Mr. Hunter knew that he was not going to discover a treasure-trove, but he was sure he was going to find something very interesting. So he began digging with all his vigour. Only about eighteen inches below the surface the blade struck against some hard substance. Mr. Hunter looked up. The apparition had vanished.

Mr. Hunter dug on and discovered that the hard substance was a human hand with the fingers and everything intact. As expected, the flesh had gone, only the bones remained. Mr. Hunter picked up the bones and knew exactly what to do.

He returned to the house, dressed himself up in his cycling costume and rode away with the bones and the spade to the cemetery. He waked the night watchman, got the gate opened, found out the tomb of the murdered woman and, close to it, interred the bones, that he had found in such a mysterious fashion, reciting as much of the service as he could remember. Then he paid some *buksheesh* (reward) to the night watchman and came home.

He put back the spade in its old place and retired. A few days after he paid a visit to the cemetery in the day-time and found that grass had grown on the spot which he had dug up. The bones had evidently not been disturbed.

The next year on the twenty-first September Mr. Hunter kept up the whole night, but he had no visit from the ghostly lady.

The house is now in the occupation of another European gentleman who took it after Mr. Hunter's transfer from the station and this new tenant had no visit from the ghost either. Let us hope that "*she*" now rests in peace.

––––––––

The following extract from a Bengal newspaper that appeared in September 1913, is very interesting and instructive.

"The following extraordinary phenomenon took place at the Hooghly Police Club Building*, Chinsurah, at about midnight on last Saturday.

"At this late hour of the night some peculiar sounds of agony on the roof of the house aroused the resident members of the Club, who at once proceeded to the roof with lamps and found to their entire surprise a lady clad in white jumping from the roof to the ground (about a hundred feet in height) followed by a man with a dagger in his hands. But eventually no trace of it could be found on the ground. This is not the first occasion that such beings are found to visit this house and it is heard from a reliable source that long ago a woman committed suicide by hanging and it is believed that her spirit loiters round the building. As these incidents have made a deep impression upon the members, they have decided to remove the Club from the said buildings."

––––––––

* Private building used for a Police Club, i.e. a type of social club for police forces.

The Morning Star by Gaganendranath Tagore, mid-1920s.

THE OPEN DOOR.

HERE again is something that is very peculiar but not very uncommon. We, myself and three other friends of mine, were asked by another friend of ours to pass a week's holiday at the suburban residence of the last named. We took an evening train after the office hours and reached our destination at about 10.30 at night. The place was about sixty miles from Calcutta.

Our host had a very large house with a number of disused wings. I do not think many of my readers have any idea of a large residential house in Bengal. Generally it is a quadrangular sort of thing with a big yard in the centre which is called the "*Angan*" or "*uthan*" (a court-yard). On all sides of the court-yard are rooms of all sorts of shapes and sizes. There are generally two stories—the lower used as kitchen, godown*, store-room, etc., and the upper as bedrooms, etc.

Now this particular house of our friend was of the kind described above. It stood on extensive grounds wooded by fruit and timber trees. There was also a big tank, a miniature lake in fact, which was the property of my friend. There was good fishing in the lake and that was the particular attraction that had drawn my other friends to this place. I myself was not very fond of angling.

As I have said we reached this place at about 10.30 at night. We were received very kindly by the father and the mother of our host who were a jolly old couple; and after a very late supper, or, shall I call it dinner, we retired. The guest rooms were well furnished and very comfortable. It was a bright moonlight night and our plan was to get up at four in the morning and go to the lake for angling.

At three in the morning the servants of our host woke us up (they had come to carry our fishing gear) and we went to the lake which was a couple of hundred yards from the house. As mentioned above it was a bright moonlight night in summer and the outing was not unpleasant after all. We remained on the bank of the lake till about seven in the morning, when one of the servants came to fetch us for our morning tea. I may as well mention here that breakfast in India generally means a pretty heavy meal at about ten in the morning.

---

* Warehouse or storage area (often for bulk goods).

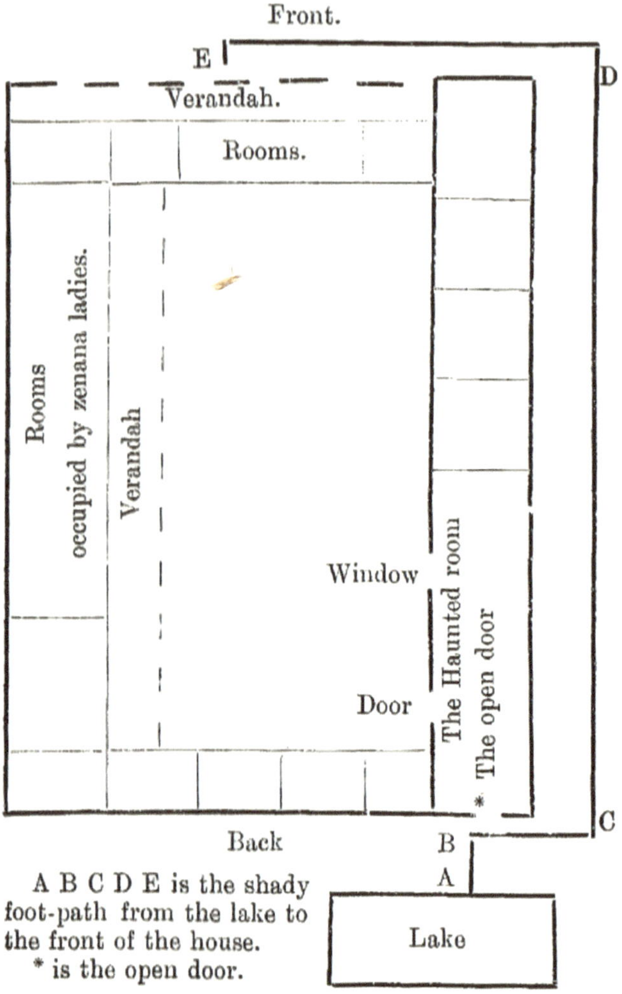

Original plan illustration for "The Open Door."

I was the first to get up; for I have already admitted that I was not a worthy disciple of Izaak Walton[*]. So I wound up my line and walked away, carrying my rod myself.

The lake was towards the back of the house. To come from the lake to the front of it we had, therefore, to pass along the whole length of the buildings. See rough plan (above).

As would appear from the plan we had to walk along the shady foot-

---

[*] Notable biographer, fisherman, and author of *The Compleat Angler*.

path ABCDE, where there was a turning at each point B, C, D and E. The back row of rooms was used for godowns, store-rooms, kitchens, etc. One of them—the one with a door marked " * " at the corner, was used for storing a number of door-frames. The owner of the house, our host's father, had at one time contemplated adding a new wing and for that purpose the door-frames had been made. Then he gave up the idea and the door-frames were stowed away in that room with a door on the outside marked " * ". Now as I was walking ahead I reached the turning B first of all, and it was probably an accident that the point of my rod touched the door. The door flew open. I knew this was an unused portion of the house and so the opening of the door surprised me to a certain extent. I looked into the room and discovered the wooden door-frames. There was nothing peculiar about the room or its contents either.

When we were drinking our tea five minutes later I casually remarked that they would find some of the door-frames missing as the door of the room in which they were kept had been left open all night. I did not at that time attach any importance to a peculiar look in the eyes of the old couple, my host's father and mother. The old gentleman called one of the servants and ordered him to bolt that door.

When we were going to the lake in the evening I examined the door and found that it had been closed from within.

The next morning we went out a-fishing again; and when we were returning for our tea, at about seven in the morning, I was again ahead of all the rest. As I came along, this time I intentionally gave a push to the door with my rod. It again flew open. "This is funny," I thought.

At tea I reported the matter to the old couple and I then noticed with curiosity their embarrassed look of the day before. I therefore suggested that the servants purposely omitted to bolt the outer door and one morning they would find the door-frames, stored in the room, gone.

At this the old man smiled. He said that the door of this particular room had remained in that condition for the last fifteen years and the contents had never been disturbed. On our pressing him to explain why the door was not properly shut at night he admitted with great reluctance that since the death of a certain servant of the household in that particular room fifteen years ago all attempts to keep the door bolted at night had proved futile. "You may shut it yourself and see," suggested the old gentleman.

We required no further invitation. Immediately we all went to that room to investigate the matter and find out the ghost if he remained indoors during the day. But Mr. Ghost was not there. "He has gone out for his morning constitutional," I suggested, "and this time we shall keep him out." Now this particular room had two doors and one window; and by this window and one of the doors the room communicated with the inner court-yard. The other door led to the grounds outside and that was the haunted door. We opened both the doors and the window and examined the room minutely. There was nothing extraordinary about it. Then we tried to close the haunted door; but found that having probably remained open for so many years, it had warped considerably. It had two very strong bolts on the inside but the lower bolt would not go within even three inches of its socket. The upper one was very loose and a little continuous thumping would bring the bolt down. We thought we had solved the mystery thus:—The servants only closed the door by pushing up the top bolt at night, and the wind would shake the door and the bolt would come down. So this time we took good care to use the lower bolt. Three of us pushed the door with all our might and one man thrust the lower bolt into its socket. It hardly went in a quarter of an inch, but still the door was secure. We then hammered the bolt in with bricks; and in doing this we broke about half a dozen of them. This will explain to the reader how much strength it required to drive the bolt in about an inch and a half.

Then we satisfied ourselves that the bolt could not be moved without the aid of a hammer and a lever. Afterwards we tightly closed the window and the other door, and securely locked the last, thus taking every precaution to prevent any human being from opening the haunted door.

Before going to bed after dinner we further examined both the doors once more. They were all right.

The next morning we did not go out for fishing so when we got up at about five in the morning the first thing we did was to go and examine the haunted door. It flew in at the mere touch as before. We then went inside and examined the other door as well as the window which opened into the court-yard. The window was as secure as we had left it and the door was chained from outside. We also went round into the court-yard and examined the lock. It did not appear to have been tampered with.

The old man and his wife met us at tea as usual. They had evidently been told everything. They, however, did not mention the subject, neither did we.

It was my intention to pass a night in that room but nobody would agree to bear me company, and I did not quite like the idea of passing a whole night in that ugly room all alone. Moreover my hosts would not have heard of it.

The mystery of the open door has not yet been solved. It was about twenty years ago that what I have narrated above, happened. I am not sure that the mystery will ever be solved.

In this connection it will not be out of place to mention another incident with regard to another family and another house in another part of Bengal.

Once while coming back from Darjeeling, the summer capital[*] of Bengal, I had a very garrulous old gentleman for a fellow traveller in the same compartment. I was reading a copy of the *Occult Review* and the title of the magazine interested him very much. He asked me what the magazine was about, and I told him. He then asked me if I was really interested in ghosts and their stories. I told him that I was.

"In our village we have a gentleman who has a family ghost," said my companion.

"What sort of thing is a family ghost?" I asked.

"Oh—the ghost comes and has his dinner with my neighbour every night," said my companion.

"Really—must be a very funny ghost and a clever one too," I remarked. "It is a fact—if you stay for a day in my village you will learn everything."

I at once decided to break my journey in the village. It was about two in the afternoon when I got down at the Railway Station—procured a hackney carriage[†] and, ascertaining the name and address of the gentleman who had the family ghost, parted company with my fellow traveller.

I reached the house in twenty minutes, and told the gentleman that I was a stranger in those parts and as such craved leave to pass the rest of the day and the night under his roof. I was a very unwelcome guest, but he could not kick me out, as the moral code would not permit it. He, however, shrewdly guessed why I was so anxious to pass the night at his house.

But all the same, my host was very kind to me. He was a tolerably rich man with a large family. Most of his sons were grown-up young men who were at College in Calcutta. The younger children were of course at home.

At night when we sat down to dinner I gently broached the subject by hinting at the rumour I had heard that his house was haunted. I further explained to him that I had only come to ascertain if what I had heard was

---

[*] Ruling classes would migrate to an alternate capital city in times of severe weather such as a cooler climate during high summer; an act done prior to modernized indoor heating and air conditioning.

[†] Carriage or car for hire, i.e. a type of independent taxi.

true. He told me (of course it was very kind of him) that the story about the dinner was false, and what really happened was this:—

"I had a younger brother who died two years ago. He was of a religious turn of mind and passed his time in reading religious books and writing articles about religion in papers. He died suddenly one night. In fact he was found dead in his bed in the morning. The doctors said it was due to failure of heart. Since his death he has come and slept in the room, which was his when he was alive and is his still. All that he takes is a glass of water fetched from our sacred river the Ganges. We put the glass of water in the room and make the bed every evening; the next morning the glass is found empty and the bed appears to have been slept in."

"But why did you begin?—" I asked.

"Oh—One night he appeared to me in a dream and asked me to keep the water and a clean bed in the room—this was about a month after his death," said my host.

"Has anybody ever passed a night in the room to see what really happens?" I asked.

"His young wife—or rather widow passed a night in that room—the next morning we found her on the bed—sleeping—dead—from failure of heart—so the doctors said."

"Most painful though interesting," I remarked.

"Nobody has gone to that part of the house since the death of the poor young widow," continued my host. "I have got all the doors of the room securely screwed up except one, and that too is kept carefully locked, and the key is always with me."

After dinner my host took me to the haunted room. All arrangements for the night were being made; and the bed was neat and clean.

A glass of the Ganges water was kept in a corner with a cover on it. I looked at the doors, they were all perfectly secure. The only door that could open was then closed and locked.

My host smiled at me sadly. "We won't do all this uselessly," he added. "This is a very costly trick if you think it a trick at all, because I have to pay to the servants double the amount that others pay in this village—otherwise they would run away. You can sleep at the door and see that nobody gets in at night."

I replied, "I believe you most implicitly and need not take the precaution suggested." I was then shown into my room and everybody withdrew.

My room was four or five apartments off, and of course these apartments were to be unoccupied.

As soon as my host and the servants had withdrawn, I took up my candle and went to the locked door of the ghostly room. With the lighted candle I covered the back of the lock with a thin coating of soot or lamp-black. Then I scraped off a little dried-up whitewash from the wall and sprinkled the powder over the lamp-black.

"If any body disturbs the lock at night I shall know it in the morning," I thought. Well, the reader could guess that I had not a good sleep that night. I got up at about 4.30 in the morning and went to the locked door. *My seal* was intact, that is, the lamp-black with the powdered lime was there just as I had left it.

I took out my handkerchief and wiped the lock clean. The whole operation took me about five minutes. Then I waited.

At about five my host came and a servant with him. The locked door was opened in my presence. The glass of water was perfectly dry and there was not a drop of water left. The bed had been slept in. There was a distinct mark on the pillow where the head should have been—and the sheet too looked as if somebody had been in bed the whole night.

I left the same day by the after-noon train having passed about twenty-three hours with the family in the haunted house.

Extract of painting from uncredited Nathadwara artist, c. 1850.

Rabindranath by Gaganendranath Tagore, mid-1920s.

WHAT UNCLE SAW.

THIS story need not have been written. It is too sad and too mysterious, but since reference has been made to it in this book, it is only right that readers should know this sad account.

Uncle was a very strong and powerful man and used to boast a good deal of his strength. He was employed in a Government Office in Calcutta. He used to come to his village home during the holidays. He was a widower with one or two children, who stayed with his brother's family in the village.

Uncle has had no bedroom of his own since his wife's death. Whenever he paid us a visit one of us used to place his bedroom at uncle's disposal. It is a custom in Bengal to sleep with one's wife and children in the same bedroom. So whenever Uncle turned up I used to vacate my bedroom for him as I was the only person without children. On such occasions I slept in one of the "*Baithaks*" (drawing-rooms). A *Baithak* is a drawing-room and guest-room combined.

In rich Bengal families of the orthodox style the "*Baithak*" or "*Baithak khana*" is a very large room generally devoid of all furniture, having only a thick rich carpet on the floor with a clean sheet upon it and big *takias* (pillows) all around the wall. The elderly people would sit on the ground and lean against the *takias*; while we, the younger lot, sat upon the *takias* and leaned against the wall which in the case of the particular room in our house was covered with some kind of yellow paint which did not come off on the clothes.

Sometimes a *takia* would burst and the cotton stuffing inside would come out; and then the old servant (his status is that of an English butler, his duty to prepare the *hookah*[*] for the master) would give us a chase with a *lathi* (stick) and the offender would run away, and not return until all incriminating evidence had been removed and the old servant's wrath had subsided.

Well, when Uncle used to come I slept in the *baithak* and my wife slept somewhere in the *zenana*[†], I never inquired where.

On this particular occasion Uncle missed the train by which he usually came. It was the month of October and he should have arrived at 8 P.M. My

---

[*] Waterpipe used to smoke tobacco or types of drugs (often vaporized) such as hashish.
[†] Section of household reserved only for women.

bed had been made in the *baithak*. But the 8 P.M. train came and stopped and passed on and Uncle did not turn up.

So we thought he had been detained for the night. It was the Durga pooja[*] season and some presents for the children at home had to be purchased and, we supposed this was what was detaining him. Accordingly at about 10 P.M. we all retired. But the bed that had been made for me in the *baithak* remained there for Uncle in case he turned up by the 11 P.M. train. As a matter of fact we did not expect him till the next morning.

But as misfortune would have it Uncle did arrive by the eleven o'clock train.

All the household had retired, and though the old servant suggested that I should be waked up, Uncle would not hear of it. He would sleep in the bed originally made for me, he said.

The bed was in the central *baithak* or hall. My Uncle was very fond of sleeping in side-rooms. I do not know why. Anyhow he ordered the servant to remove his bed to one of the side-rooms. Accordingly the bed was taken to one of them. One side of that room had two windows overlooking a garden. This garden was more a park-like place, rather neglected, but still well wooded abounding in jack fruit trees. So it used to be quite shady and dark there even during the day. On this particular night it must have been very dark indeed. I do not remember now whether there was a moon or not.

Well, Uncle went to sleep and so did the servants. It was about eight o'clock the next morning, when we thought that Uncle had slept long enough, that we went to wake him up.

The door connecting the side-room with the main *baithak* was closed, but not bolted from inside; so we pushed the door open and went in.

Uncle lay in bed panting. He stared at us with eyes that did not perceive. We at once knew that something was wrong, and on touching his body we found that he had high fever. We opened the windows, and it was then that Uncle spoke, "Don't open or it would come in—"

"What would come in, Uncle—what?" we asked.

But uncle had fainted.

The doctor was called in. He arrived at about ten in the morning. He said it was high fever—due to what he could not say. All the same he prescribed a medicine.

---

[*] Festival and celebration of Durga, the Hindu goddess of strength, motherhood, and wars; protective mother of the universe.

The medicine had the effect of reducing the temperature, and at about six in the evening consciousness returned. But he was still in a very weak condition. Some medicine was given to induce sleep and he passed the night well. We nursed him by turns at night, and the next morning we had the satisfaction of seeing him all right. He walked from the bedroom, though still very weak and came to the central *baithak* where he had tea with us. It was then that we asked what he had seen and what he had meant by "It would come in."

Oh! how we wish we had never asked him the question, at least then.

This was what he said:—

"After I had gone to bed I found that there were a few mosquitoes and so I could not sleep well. It was about midnight when they gradually disappeared and then I began to fall asleep. But just as I was dozing off I heard somebody strike the bars of the windows thrice. It was like three distinct strokes with a cane on the gratings outside. 'Who is there?' I asked; but no reply. The striking stopped. Again I closed my eyes and again the same strokes were repeated. This time I nearly lost my temper; I thought it was some urchin of the neighbourhood in a mischievous mood. 'Who is there?' I again shouted—again no reply. The striking however stopped. But after a time it commenced afresh. This time I lost my temper completely and opened the window, determined to thrash anybody whom I might find there—forgetting that the windows were barred and fully six feet above the ground. Well in the darkness I saw, I saw—."

Here uncle had a fit of shivering and panting, and within a minute he lost all consciousness. The fever was again high. The doctor was summoned but this time his medicines did no good. Uncle never regained consciousness and in spite of the unremitting efforts of the doctor for twenty-four hours he died of heart failure the next morning, leaving his story unfinished he died of heart failure the next morning, leaving his story unfinished and without our having the least inkling of what that terrible thing was which he had seen beyond the window. The whole thing remains a deep mystery and unfortunately the mystery will never be solved.

Nobody has ventured to pass a night in the side-room since then. If I had not been a married man with a very young wife I might have tried.

One thing however remains and it is this that though uncle got all the fright in the world in that room, he neither came out of that room nor called for help. One cry for help and the whole household would have been awake. In fact there was a servant within thirty yards of the window which uncle had opened; and this man says he heard uncle open the window and close and bolt it again, though he had not heard uncle's shouts of "Who is there?"

Only this morning I read this funny advertisement in the *Morning Post*.

"*Haunted Houses.*—Man and wife, cultured and travelled, gentle people—having lost fortune ready to act as care-takers and to investigate in view of removing trouble—."

Well—in a haunted house these gentle people expect to see something. Let us hope they will not see what our Uncle saw or what the Major saw.

This advertisement, however, clearly shows that even in countries like England, haunted houses do exist, or at least houses exist which are believed to be haunted.

If what we see really depends on what we think or what we believe, no wonder that there are so many more haunted houses in India than in England. This reminds me of a very old incident of my early school days. A boy was really caught by a Ghost and then there was trouble. We shall not forget the thrashing we received from our teacher in the school; and the fellow who was actually caught by the Ghost—if Ghost it was, will never say in future that Ghosts don't exist.

In this connection it may not be out of place to narrate another incident, though it does not fall within the same category with the main story that heads this chapter. The only reason why I do so is that the facts tally in one respect, though in one respect only, and that is that the person who knew would tell nothing.

This was a friend of mine who was a widower. We were in the same office together and he occupied a chair and a table next but one to mine. This gentleman was in our office for six months only after he had narrated the story. If he had stayed longer we might have got out his secret, but unfortunately he went away; he has gone so far from us that probably we shall not meet again for the next ten years.

It was in connection with the "Smith's dead wife's photograph" controversy that one day one of my fellow clerks told me that a visit from a dead wife was nothing very wonderful, as our friend Haralal could testify.

I always took of a lot of interest in ghosts and their stories. So I was generally at Haralal's desk cross-examining him about this affair; at first the gentleman was very uncommunicative but when he saw I would give him no rest he made a statement which I have every reason to believe is true. This is more or less what he says.

"It was about ten years ago that I joined this office. I have been a widower ever since I left college—in fact I married the daughter of a neighbour when I was at college and she died about three years afterwards, when I was just thinking of beginning life in right earnest. She has been dead these ten years and I shall never marry again. (A young widower in good circumstances, in Bengal, is as rare as a blue rose˙).

"I have a suite of bachelor rooms in Calcutta, but I go to my suburban home on every Saturday afternoon and stay there till Monday morning, thus I pass the week end regularly at home all the year round.

"On this particular occasion nearly eight years ago, that is, about a year and a half after the death of my young wife I went home by an evening train. There is any number of trains in the evening and there is no certainty by which train I may go, so if I am late, generally everybody goes to bed with the exception of my mother.

"On this particular night I reached home rather late. It was the month of September and there had been a heavy shower in the town and all tram-car services had been suspended.

"When I reached the Railway Station I found that the trains were not running to time either. I was given to understand that a tree had been blown down against the telegraph wire, and so the signals were not going through; and as it was rather dark the trains were only running on the report of *a motor trolly* that the line was clear. Thus I reached home at about eleven instead of eight in the evening.

"I found my father also sitting up for me though he had had his dinner. He wanted to learn the particulars of the storm at Calcutta.

"Within ten minutes of my arrival he went to bed and within an hour I finished my dinner and retired for the night.

"It was rather stuffy and the bed was damp as I was perspiring freely; and consequently I was not feeling inclined to sleep.

"A little after midnight I felt that there was somebody else in the room.

"I looked at the closed door—yes there was no mistake about it, it was my wife, my wife who had been dead these eighteen months.

"At first I was—well you can guess my feeling—then she spoke:

˙ Highly sought and often socially expected (sometimes compulsory) for widowers to remarry; the opposite for widows, who were frequently turned outcasts.

"'There is a cool bed-mat under the bedstead; it is rather dusty, but it will make you comfortable.

"I got up and looked under the bedstead—yes the cool bed-mat was there right enough and it was dusty too. I took it outside and I cleaned it by giving it a few jerks, and then involuntarily exclaimed 'When pain and anguish wring the brow, A ministering angel thou'*—Yes, I had to pass through the door at which she was standing within six inches of her,—don't put any questions. Let me tell you as much as I like; you will get nothing out of me if you interrupt—yes, I passed a comfortable night. She was in that room for a long time, telling me lots of things. The next morning my mother enquired with whom I was talking and I told her a lie. I said I was reading my novel aloud. But they all know it at home now. She comes and passes two nights with me in the week when I am at home. She does not come to Calcutta. She talks about various matters and she is happy—don't ask me how I know that. I shall not tell you whether I have touched her body because that will give rise to further questions.

"Everybody at home has seen her, and they all know what I have told you, but nobody has spoken to her. They all respect and love her—nobody is afraid. In fact she never comes except on Saturday and Sunday evenings and that when I am at home."

No amount of cross-examination, coaxing or inducement made my friend Haralal say anything further.

This story, in itself, would not have probably gained credence; but after the incident of "His dead wife's picture" nobody doubted its credibility. And there is no reason why anybody should; for Haralal is not a man who would tell yarns; besides I have made enquiries at Haralal's village where several persons know this much, that his dead wife pays him a visit twice every week.

Now that Haralal is five hundred miles from his village home I do not know how things stand; but I am told that this story reached the ears of the *Bara Saheb*[†] and he asked Haralal if he would object to a transfer and Haralal told him that he would not.

I shall leave the reader to draw his own conclusions.

---

[*] From "Marmion" by Sir Walter Scott (Canto 6, St. 30): "ministering angel" meaning a virtuous and helpful wife; also the idea of women ministering to male needs.

[†] Hindi designation for the head British administrator in a given locality; somewhat slang as "big boss."

Uncredited illustration of an Indian clerk, titled
"Zamidar, a Bengalese Babu," ca. 1907.

Uncredited 1882 wood engraving depicting the
act of cremation at a *ghat* in Calcutta, India.

THE BOY WHO WAS CAUGHT.

NOTHING is more common in India than seeing a ghost. Every one of us has seen ghost at some period of his existence; and if we have not actually seen one, some other person has, and has given us such a vivid description that we cannot but believe to be true what we hear.

This is, however, my own experience. I am told others have observed the phenomenon before.

When we were boys at school we used, among other things, to discuss ghosts. Most of my fellow students asserted that they did not believe in ghosts, but I was one of those who not only believed in their existence but also in their power to do harm to human beings if they liked. Naturally, I was in the minority; though as a matter of fact I knew that all those who said that they did not believe in ghosts told a lie. They too believed in ghosts as much as I did, only they had not the courage to admit their weakness and differ boldly from the sceptics. Among the lot of unbelievers was one Ram Lal, a student of the Fifth Standard[*], who swore that he did not believe in ghosts and further that he would do anything to convince us that they did not exist.

It was, therefore, at my suggestion that he decided to go one moonlight night and hammer down a wooden peg[†] into the soft sandy soil of the Hindoo Burning *Ghat*[‡], it being well known that the ghosts generally put in a visible appearance at a burning *ghat* on a moonlight night. (A burning *ghat* is the place where dead bodies of Hindoos are cremated).

It was the warm month of April and the river had shrunk into the size of a *nullah*[§] or drain. The real *pukka ghat*[**] (the bathing place built of bricks and lime) was, therefore, about two hundred yards from the water of the main stream, with a stretch of sand between.

The *ghats* are ordinarily used only in the morning when people come to bathe, and in the evening they are generally all deserted. So after a game of

---

[*] Fifth grade, elementary school.

[†] Stake.

[‡] Similar to a quay; stone steps leading down to bathing wharves or cremation places (alongside a river or pool's banks).

[§] Riverbed at bottom of valley or ravine that is mostly dry.

[**] *Pukka*, meaning *actual,* the "real" ghat; i.e. because the river was so shrunken the ghat, which should have been alongside it, was actually two hundred yards away.

football* on the school grounds we frequently used to resort to the *pukka ghat* on sultry days and stay there for an hour or so and then return home after nightfall.

Now, it was the twenty-third of April and a bright moonlight night; every one of us (there were about a dozen) had told the people at home that there was a function at the school and he might be late. On this night, it was arranged that the ghost test should take place.

The boy who had challenged the ghost, Ram Lal, was to join us at the *pukka ghat* at 8 P.M.; and then while we waited there he would walk across the sand and drive the peg into the ground at the place where a dead body had been cremated that very morning. We were to supply the peg and the hammer. (I had to pay the school gardener two annas† for the loan of a peg and a hammer).

Well, we procured the peg and the hammer and proceeded to the *pukka ghat*. If the gardener had known what we required the peg and the hammer for, I am sure he would not have lent these to us.

Though I was a firm believer in ghosts yet I did not expect that Ram Lal would be caught. What I hoped for was that he would not turn up at the trysting place. But to my disappointment Ram Lal did turn up and at the appointed hour too. He came boasting as usual, took the peg and the hammer and started across the sand saying that he would break the head of any ghost who might venture within the reach of the hammerhead. Well, he went along and we waited for his return at the *pukka ghat*. It was a glorious night, the whole expanse of sand was shining in the bright moonlight.

On and on went Ram Lal with the peg in his left hand and the hammer in his right. He was dressed in the usual upcountry Indian style, in a long coat or *Achkan*‡ which reached well below his knees and fluttered in the breeze.

As he went on, his pace slackened. When he had gone about half the distance he stopped and looked back. We hoped he would return. He put down the hammer and the peg, sat down on the sand facing us, took off his shoes. Only some sand had got in. He took up the peg and hammer and walked on.

But then we felt that his courage was oozing away. Another fifty yards and he again stopped, and looked back at us.

Another fifty yards remained. Will he return? No! he again proceeded, but we could clearly see that his steps were less jaunty than when he had

---

* Soccer, for American readers.

† Former unit of currency in British India; one anna equaled 1/16 of a rupee.

‡ High-collared, knee-length jacket generally worn over a *kurta* (long shirt or tunic).

started. We knew that he was trembling, we knew that he would have blessed us to call him back. But we would not yield, neither would he. Looking in our direction at every step he proceeded and reached the burning *ghat*. He reached the identical spot where the pyre had been erected in the morning.

Here there was a perfect calm—no breeze,—not a mouse stirring. Not a soul was within two hundred yards of him and he could not expect much help from us. How poor Ram Lal's heart must have palpitated! When we see Ram Lal now how we feel that we should burst.

Well, Ram Lal knelt down, fixed the peg in the wet sandy soil and began hammering. After each stroke he looked at us and at the river and in all directions. He struck blow after blow and we counted about thirty. That his hands had become nerveless we would understand, for otherwise a dozen strokes should have been enough to make the peg vanish in the soft sandy soil.

The peg went in and only about a couple of inches remained visible above the surface; and then Ram Lal thought of coming back. He was kneeling still. He tried to stand up, gave out a shrill cry for help and fell down face foremost.

It must have been his cry for help that made us forget our fear of the ghost, and we all ran at top speed towards the *ghat*. It was rather difficult to run fast on the sand but we managed it as best we could, and stopped only when we were about half a dozen yards from the prostrate form of Ram Lal.

There he lay unconscious as if gone to sleep. Our instinct told us that he was not dead. We thanked God, and each one of us sent up a silent prayer. Then we cried for help and a boatman who lived a quarter of a mile away came up. He took up Ram Lal in his arms and as he was doing so *tr—rrrrrrrrrr—* went Ram Lal's long coat. The unfortunate lad had hammered the skirt of his long coat along with the peg into the ground.

We took Ram Lal to his house and explained to his mother how he had a bad fall in the football field, and there we left him.

The next morning at school, one student, who was a neighbour of Ram Lal, told us that the whole mischief had become known.

Ram Lal, it appears, got high fever immediately after we had left him and about midnight he became delirious and in that condition he disclosed everything in connection with his adventure at the *ghat*.

In the evening we went to see him. His parents, as expected, were very angry with us.

The whole story reached the ears of the school authorities and we got, what I thought we richly deserved (for having allowed a mere mortal to defy a ghost) but what I need not say.

Ram Lal is now a grown-up young man. He holds a responsible government appointment and I meet him sometimes when he comes to tour in our part of the Province. I always ask him if he has seen a ghost since we met last.

In this connection it will not be out of place to mention two simple stories one from my own experience and another told by a friend.

I shall tell my friend's story first, in his own words.

"I used to go for a bath in the Ganges early every morning. I used to start from home at four o'clock in the morning and walked down to the Ganges which was about three miles from my house. The bath took about an hour and then I used to come back in my carriage which went for me at about six in the morning.

"On this eventful morning when I awoke it was brilliant moonlight and so I mistook it for the peep of dawn.

"I, accordingly, started from home without looking at the clock and when I was about a mile and a half from home and about the same distance from the river I realized that I was rather early. The policeman under the railway bridge told me that it was only two o'clock. I knew that I should have to cross the small *maidan** through which the road lay and I remembered that there was a rumour that a ghost had sometimes been seen in the *maidan* and on the road. This however did not make me nervous, because I really did not believe in ghosts; all the same I wished I could have gone back. But then in going back I should have to pass the policeman and he would think that I was afraid; so I decided to go on.

"When I entered the *maidan* a creepy sensation came over me. My first idea was that I was being followed, and though I did not care to look back, nevertheless I went on with quicker steps.

"My next idea was that a gust of wind swept past me, and then I thought that a huge form was passing, from the opposite direction, over the trees which skirted the road.

"By this time I was in the middle of the *maidan* about half a mile from the nearest human being.

"And then, horror of horrors, the huge form came down from the trees and stood in the middle of the road about a hundred yards ahead of me, barring my way.

"I instinctively moved to the side—but did not stop. By the time that spot was reached, I had left the metalled portion of the road and was actually

---

* Large open space used for ceremonial occasions, parades, etc.; often so immense as to be sectioned off into multiple areas such as parks, sports fields, etc.

passing under the road-side trees prudently allowing their thick trunks to intervene between me and the huge form standing in the middle of the road. I did not look at it, but I was sure it was extending a gigantic arm towards me. It could not, however, catch me and I walked on with vigorous strides. After I had passed the figure I began almost to run fast under the trees, my heart beating like a sledge hammer within me, with fear and exertion.

"After a couple of minutes I saw two glaring eyes in front of me. This I thought was the end. The eyes were advancing towards me at a rapid pace and then I heard a shout like that of a cow in distress. I stopped where I was, and hoped the ghost would pass along the road overlooking me. But when the ghost was within say fifty yards of me it gave another howl and I knew that it had seen me. A cry for help escaped my lips and I fainted.

"When I regained consciousness I found myself on the grassy foot-path by the side of the road, with four or five human beings hovering over and about me and a motor car standing near.

"Then the whole mystery became clear as day-light. The eyes that I had seen were the headlights of the 24 H.P. Silent Knight Minerva* of Captain——. He had gone on a pleasure-trip to the next station and was returning home with two friends and his wife in his motor car. When in that part of the road he saw something like a man standing in the middle of it and sounded his horn. But as the figure in the middle of the road would not move aside he slowed down and then heard my cry.

"The rest the reader may guess. The figure that had loomed so large with out-stretched arm was only a municipal danger signal erected in the middle of the road. A red lamp had been placed on the top of the erection but it had been blown out."

This was the whole story of my friend. It shows how even our prosaic but overwrought imagination sometimes gives to airy nothings a local habitation and a name.

My own personal experience which I shall describe now will also, I am sure, be interesting.

It was on a brilliant moonlight night in the month of June that we were sleeping in the open court-yard of our house.

As usual, the court-yard had a wall all round with a partition in the middle; on one side of the partition slept three girls of the family and on the other were the younger male members, four in number.

---

* Brand of high-end Knight engine (by Charles Yale Knight) known for its noiselessness, driven in a Minerva (Belgian manufacturer of luxury cars) automobile. Both Knight and Minerva were out of business by the mid-1900s.

It was our custom to have a long chat after dinner and before retiring to bed. On this particular night the talk had been about ghosts. Of course, the girls are always ready to believe everything supernatural and so when we left them we knew that they would not sleep very comfortably that night. We retired to our part of the court-yard, but we could overhear the conversation of the girls. One was trying to convince the other two that ghosts did not exist and if they did exist they never came into contact with human beings. Then we fell asleep.

How long we had slept we did not know, but a sudden cry from one of the girls awoke us and within three seconds we were across the low partition wall and with her. She was sitting up in bed pointing with her fingers. Following the direction we saw in the clear moonlight the figure of a short woman standing in the corner of the court-yard about twenty yards from us pointing her finger at something (not towards us). We then looked in that direction but could see nothing peculiar there.

Our first idea was that it was one of the maidservants, who had heard our after-dinner conversation, was playing the ghost. But this particular ghostly lady was very short, much shorter than any servant in the establishment. After some hesitation all (four) of us advanced towards the ghost. I remember how my heart throbbed as I advanced with the other three boys.

Then we laughed loud and long.

What do you think it was that greeted our eyes?

It was only the Lawn Tennis net wrapped round the pole standing against the wall. The handle of the ratchet arrangement looked like an extending finger. But from a distance in the moonlight the whole thing seemed to have assumed the likeness of a short woman draped in white.

Talking of ghosts reminds me of a very funny story told by a friend of my grandfather—a famous medical man of Calcutta.

This famous doctor was once sent for to treat a gentleman at Agra. This gentleman was a rich Marwari who was suffering from indigestion. When the doctor reached Agra he was lodged in very comfortable quarters and a number of horses and carriages were placed at his disposal.

He was informed that the patient had been treated by all the local and provincial practitioners but without any result.

The doctor who was as clever a man of the world as of medicine, at once saw that there was really nothing the matter with the patient. He was only suffering from a curious malady which could in a phrase be called—"want of physical exercise."

Agra, "the Imperial city of Akbar," after which the Province is now named, abounds in magnificent old buildings and picturesque sights which it takes the tourist a considerable time to visit; and the Doctor was, of course, seeing the lions of the place and enjoying their architectural beauty with the aid of a cicerone[*].

He had in the meantime prescribed a number of medicines which, however, proved of no avail. The Doctor had anticipated it, and so he had decided what medicine he would prescribe next.

During the sight-seeing excursions into the environs of the city the doctor had discovered a large *pukka* well not far from a main street and at a distance of three miles from his patient's house.

This was a very old disused well and it was generally rumoured that a ghost dwelt in it. So nobody would go near the well at night, specially as there was a lot of stories as to what the ghost looked like and how he came out at times and stood on the brink and all that,—but the doctor did not really believe any of these. He, however, believed that this ghost (whether there really was any or not in that well) would cure his patient.

So one morning when he saw his patient he said, "Lalla[†] Saheb—I have found out the real cause of your trouble—it is a ghost whom you have got to propitiate[‡] and unless you do that you will never get well—and no medicine will help you and your digestion will never improve."

"A Ghost?" asked the patient.

"A Ghost!" exclaimed the people around.

"A Ghost," said the doctor sagely.

"What shall I have to do?" inquired the patient, anxiously—

"You will have to go every morning to that well (indicating the one mentioned above), and throw a basketful of flowers in," said the doctor.

"I shall do that every day," promised the patient.

"Then we shall begin from tomorrow," said the doctor.

The next morning everybody had been ready long before the doctor was out of bed. He came at last and all got up to start. Then a big landau and pair[§] drew up to take the doctor and the patient to the abode of the ghost in

---

[*] Type of cultural tour guide, specializing in visiting museums, galleries, etc.

[†] Ambiguous term used in India for men of means; a gentleman, clerk, teacher, etc.

[‡] Win the favor of.

[§] Four-wheeled luxury carriage pulled by a pair of horses.

the well. Just as the patient was thinking of getting in the doctor said, "We don't require a carriage, Lalla Saheb—we shall all have to walk—and bare-footed too, and between you and me we shall have to carry the basket of flowers also."

The patient was really troubled. Never indeed in his life had he walked a mile—not to say of three—and that, bare-footed and carrying a basket of flowers in his hands. However he had to do it. It was a goodly procession. The big millionaire—the big doctor with a large number of followers walking bare-footed—caused amazement and amusement to all who saw them.

It took them a full hour and a half to reach the well—and there the doctor pronounced the *mantra* in Sanskrit and the flowers were thrown in. The *mantra* (charm) was in Sanskrit, the doctor who knew a little of the language had taken great pains to compose it the night before and even then it was not grammatically quite correct.

At last the party returned, but not on foot. The journey back was performed in the carriages that had followed the patient and his doctor. From that day the practice was followed regularly. The patient's health began to improve and he began to regain his power of digestion fast. In a month he was all right; but he never discontinued the practice of going to the well and throwing in a basketful of flowers with his own hands. He had also learnt the *mantra* (the mystic charm) by heart; but the doctor had sworn him to secrecy and he told it to nobody. Shoes with felt soles were soon procured from England (it being forty years before any Indian Rope Sole Shoe Factory came into existence) and thus the inconvenience of walking this distance bare-footed was easily obviated.

After a month's further stay the doctor came away from Agra having earned a fabulous fee, and he always received occasional letters and presents from his patient who never discontinued the practice of visiting the well till his death about seventeen years later.

"The three-mile walk is all that he requires," said the doctor to his friends (among whom evidently my grandfather was one) on his return from Agra, "and since he has got used to it now he won't discontinue even if he comes to know of the deception I have practised on him—and after all I have cured his indigestion."

The patient, of course, never discovered the fraud. He never gave the matter his serious consideration. His friends, who were as ignorant and prejudiced as he was himself, believed in the *ghost* theory as implicitly as he did. The medical practitioners of Agra who probably were in the Doctor's secret never told him anything—and if they had told him anything they would probably have heard language from *Our patient* that could not well be described as quite parliamentary, for they had all tried to cure him and failed.

This series of stories will prove how much his "imagination" works upon the external organs and physical faculties of a human being. If a person goes about with the idea that there is a ghost somewhere about he will probably see the ghost in everything.

But has it ever struck the reader that sometimes horses and dogs do not quite enjoy going to a place which is reputed to be haunted?

In a village in Bengal not very far from my home there is a big jackfruit tree which is said to be haunted.

I visited this place once—the local *zamindar*[*] had sent me his elephant. The *Gomashta* (estate-manager) who knew that I had come to see the haunted tree told me that I should probably see nothing during the day, but the elephant would not go near the tree.

I passed round this tree, which was about three miles from the Railway Station: but there was nothing extraordinary about it. As it was now about eleven o'clock in the morning I went to the Shooting Box (usually called the *Cutcherry* or Court house—where the *zamindars* and their servants put up when they pay a visit to this part of their possessions) to have my bath and breakfast most hospitably provided by my generous host. I then ordered the elephant to be taken under that tree, and this was done though the people there assured me that the elephant would not remain there long.

At about 2 P.M. an extraordinary noise seemed to proceed from the tree. But it was only the elephant. It was wailing and was looking as uncomfortable as it possibly could.

We approached nearer but found nothing terrible. The elephant too was not really ill. I, however, ordered it to be taken away from under the tree. As soon as the chain was removed from the animal's leg it rushed away with the speed of a race horse and would not stop within a quarter of a mile of the tree. I was vastly amused, for I had never seen an elephant running before. But under the tree there was nothing to scare away the beast. What made the elephant so afraid has remained a secret.

The servants told me (what I had heard before) that it was only elephants, horses and dogs that did not stay long under that tree. No human eyes have ever seen anything supernatural or fearful there.

---

[*] Large landowner; i.e. feudal ruler who leases his land to tenant farmers.

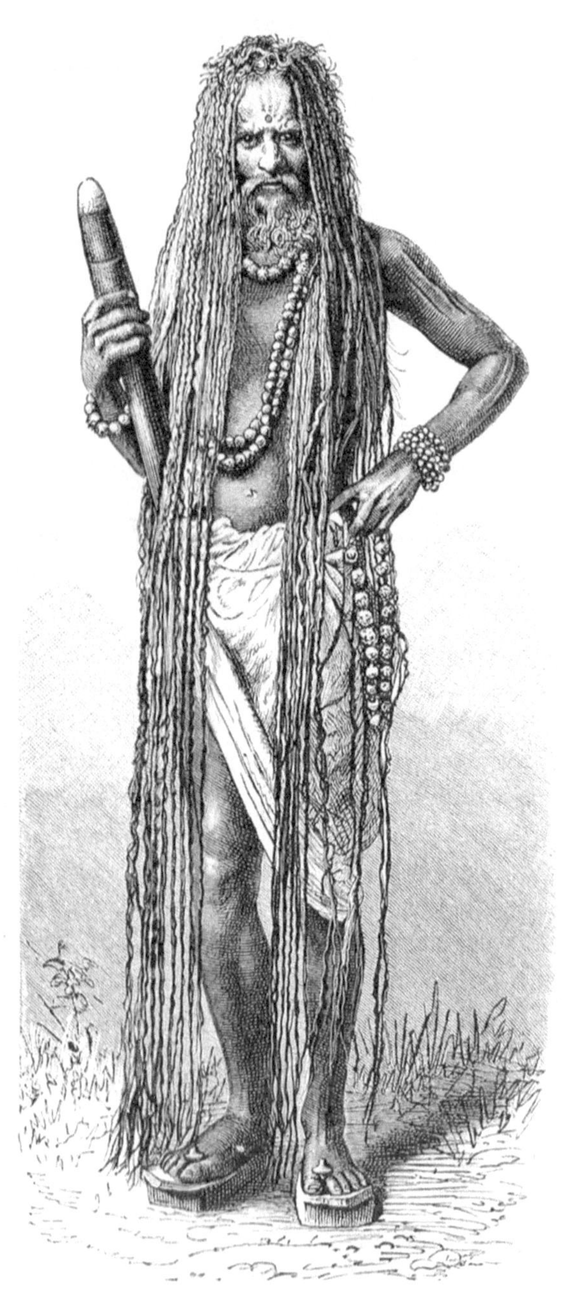

Engraved illustration of an Indian Fakir from *The History of Mankind, Vol. III*, by Professor Friedrich Ratzel (1898).

THE STARVING MILLIONAIRE.

THIS story was also in the papers. It created a sensation at the time, now it has been almost forgotten. The story shows that black art with all its mysteries is not a thing of the past.

This was what happened.

There was a certain rich European Contractor in the Central Provinces in India.

Let us call him Anderson. He used to supply stone ballast to the Railway Companies and had been doing this business for over a quarter of a century. He had accumulated wealth and was a multi-millionaire and one of the richest men in his part of the country. The district which he made his headquarters was a large one. It was a second class military station and there were two European regiments and one Indian regiment in that station. Necessarily there was a number of European military officers besides a number of civil and executive officers in that station.

On a certain June morning, which is a very hot month in India, an Indian *Fakir*[*] came into the compound of Mr. Anderson begging for alms. Mr. Anderson and his wife were sitting in the verandah drinking their morning tea. It had been a very hot night and there being no electricity in this particular station, Mr. Anderson had to depend on the sleepy *punkha coolie*[†]. The *punkha coolie* on this particular night was more sleepy than usual, and so Mr. Anderson had passed a very sleepless night indeed, and consequently, he was in a very bad mood. A whole life passed among Indian workmen does not generally make a man good-tempered, and a hot June in the Indian plains is not particularly conducive to sweet temper either. When this beggar came in Mr. Anderson was thus in a very bad mood: and as the man walked fearlessly up to the verandah, Mr. Anderson's temper became worse. He asked the beggar what he wanted. The beggar answered he wanted food. Of course, Mr. Anderson said he had nothing to give. The beggar replied that he would accept some money and buy the food. Mr. Anderson was not in the habit of being contradicted. He

---

[*] Ascetic who renounces worldly possessions and dedicates life to the worship of God (often of Muslim faith).

[†] Unskilled laborer (coolie) who would manually operate a large canvas fan known as a punkha (or punkah) to cool a room; occupation also known as a *punkah-wallah*.

lost his temper—abused the beggar and ordered his servants to turn the man out. The servants obeyed. Before his departure the beggar turned to Mr. Anderson and told him that very soon he would know how painful it was to be hungry.

When the beggar was gone Mr. Anderson thought of his last remark and laughed. He was a well-known rich man and a good paymaster. An order for a £100 on a dirty slip of paper would be honoured by his banker without hesitation. Naturally he laughed. He forgot that men had committed suicide by drowning to avoid death from thirst. Well, there it was.

The bell announcing breakfast rang punctually at ten o'clock in the morning. Mr. Anderson joined his wife in the drawing-room and they went to the dining-room together. The smell of eggs and bacon and coffee greeted them and Mr. Anderson forgot all about the Indian beggar when he took his seat. But he received a rude shock. There was a big live caterpillar in the fish. Mr. Anderson called the servant and ordered him to take away the fish and serve with eyes open the next time. The servant who had been in Mr. Anderson's service a long time stared open-mouthed. Only a minute before there was nothing but fish on the plate. Whence came this ugly creature? Well, the plate was removed and another put in its place for the next dish.

When the next dish came another surprise awaited everybody.

As the cover was removed it was found that the whole contents were covered with a thin layer of sweepings*. The *Khansama* (the house-steward who also serves the table†) looked at Mr. Anderson and Mr. Anderson at the Khansama "with a wild surmise"; the cover was replaced and the dish taken away. Nothing was said this time.

After about five minutes of waiting a third covered dish was brought.

When the cover was removed, the contents were found mixed with stable sweepings. The smell was horrible, the dish was at once removed.

This was about the limit.

No man can eat after that. Mr. Anderson left the table and went to his office—without breakfast.

It was the habit of Mr. Anderson to have his lunch in his office. A Khansama used to take a tiffin basket‡ to the office and there in his private room Mr. Anderson ate his lunch punctually at 2 P.M. Today he expected

---

* That which is swept from the ground, i.e. dirt or rubbish.
† I.e. both cook and waiter, among other duties of a male servant.
‡ Lunch basket, smaller than a picnic basket.

his tiffin early. He thought that though he had left no instructions himself the Khansama would have the sense to remember that he had come to office without breakfast. And so Mr. Anderson expected a lunch heavier than usual and earlier too.

But it was two o'clock and the servant had not arrived. Mr. Anderson was a man of particularly regular habits. He was very hungry. The thought of the beggar in the morning made him angry too. He shouted to his *punkha coolie* to pull harder.

It was a quarter after two and still the Khansama would not arrive. It was probably the first time in twenty years that the fellow was late. Mr. Anderson, therefore, sent his *chaprasi* (peon) to look for the Khansama at about half past two.

A couple of minutes after the *chaprasi's* departure, Mr. Atkins, the Collector of the district, was announced. (A Collector is generally a District Magistrate also, and in the Central Provinces he is called the Deputy Commissioner, and is one of the principal officers in the district). In this particular district of which I am speaking there were two principal government officers. The Divisional Judge was the head of the Civil Administration as well as the person who tried the murderers and all other big offenders who deserved more than seven years imprisonment. He was a Bengal Brahman*. Mr. Atkins was the Collector or rather the Deputy Commissioner, and was also the Executive head of the district. He was also the District Magistrate. Mr. Atkins came in and thus explained a sad accident which Mr. Anderson's Khansama had met with:

"As I was passing along the road in my motor car, your man came in the way and was knocked down. The man is hurt but not badly. He had been carrying a tiffin basket which was also knocked down, as a matter of course; and the car having passed over it, everything the basket contained in the shape of china was smashed up. The man has been taken to the hospital by myself in an unconscious condition, but the doctor says there is nothing very serious, and he will be all right in a couple of days."

Now Mr. Atkins was a great friend of Mr. Anderson. They had known each other ever since Mr. Atkins's arrival in India as a young member of the Civil Service. That was more than twenty years ago. He had at first been in that district for over seven years as an Assistant Commissioner and this time he was there for over three years as a Deputy Commissioner. But Mr. Anderson was

---

* Upper caste of Hindu community from the region of Bengal, perceived as educators or leaders due to caste-privilege.

very hungry, and the story of Mr. Atkins had given him the second shock since that morning. He, therefore, used language which no gentleman should have done; and with great vehemence threatened to prosecute Mr. Atkins for rash driving, etc.

Mr. Atkins was a very good-natured man. And though he had some idea of the short temper of Mr. Anderson he had never found that gentleman so angry before. He therefore beat a hasty retreat, wondering whether Mr. Anderson had not gone mad. He would not have told anybody what happened in Mr. Anderson's offices if he had known the starving condition of the millionaire, but as it happened he repeated the fine language that Mr. Anderson had used, in the club that same evening. Everybody who heard his story opined at the time that Mr. Anderson was clearly off his head.

Mr. Anderson and his wife were as usual expected at the club, but they did not turn up.

When, however, Mr. Atkins went home he got a letter from Mr. Anderson in which the latter had apologised for what he had said in the office that afternoon.

In the letter there was a sentence which was rather enigmatic:

"If you know what I am suffering from, Atkins, you will be sorry for me, not angry with me—I pray to God you may not suffer such—." The letter had evidently been written in great haste and had not been revised. Mr. Atkins did not quite understand the matter; and he intended to look up Mr. Anderson the first thing next morning. Mr. Atkins thought that Mr. Anderson had probably lost some of his money and though it was well known that Mr. Anderson never speculated, still he might have suffered a heavy loss in one of his contracts. He telephoned to Mr. Anderson at his house, but was informed by one of the servants that the master had gone out in his motor car at six in the evening and was not back till then.

Now let us see what happened to Mr. Anderson after he had left his office at about four in the afternoon.

He went home and expected some tea, but no tea arrived, though it was six. The Khansama was in the hospital; the cook was called and he humbly offered the following explanation: "As soon as *Huzoor* (Your Honour)[*] came back I ordered the *khidmatgar* (an assistant who also waits at table) to put the kettle on the fire. There was a bright coal fire in the stove, and the khidmatgar put the kettle upon it. The kettle should have boiled within five minutes, but it did not; your humble servant went to investigate the cause

---

[*] Term of respect given to people of title or high standing.

and found that there was no water in the kettle. We put in some, but the kettle had in the meantime become nearly red-hot. As soon as it came into contact with the cold water it burst like a bomb. Fortunately nobody was hurt. There was, of course, a saucepan to heat some water in, but the cold water had got into the stove and extinguished it." It would be another half an hour before tea was ready, he added. Mr. Anderson now realised that it was not the fault of the servants but the curse of the Indian Fakir. So with a sad smile he ordered his motor car and thought that he and his wife had better try the Railway Refreshment Rooms*. When his chauffeur was going to start the engine Mr. Anderson expected that there would be a backfire and the chauffeur would have a dislocated wrist. The engine, however, started as smoothly as it had never done before and Mr. and Mrs. Anderson reached the Railway Refreshment Rooms without any accident. But there they were informed that no tea was available. A dead rat had been found under one of the tables in the first class refreshment room, and as plague cases had been reported earlier in the week, the Station Master had ordered the rooms to be closed till they had been thoroughly disinfected. The whole staff of waiters with all the preserved meat and oilman's stores had been sent by special train to the next station so that the railway passengers might not be inconvenienced. The next station was eight miles off and there was no road for a motor car.

"I had expected as much," said Mr. Anderson bitterly, as he left the Railway Station.

"I would go to Captain Fraser and beg for some dinner. He is the only man who has got a family here and will be able to accommodate us," said he to his wife, and so off they started for a five-mile run to the Cantonments. There was some trouble with the car on the way and they were detained for about an hour, and it was actually 8.30 in the evening when the Andersons reached Captain Fraser's place. Why, instead of going home from the Railway Station, Mr. Anderson went to Captain Fraser's place he himself could not tell.

When the Andersons reached Captain Fraser's place at half past eight in the evening, Mr. and Mrs. Fraser had not come back from the club. But they were expected every minute. It was, however, nine when the Captain and his wife turned up in a Hackney Carriage. They were surprised to see the Andersons; for they had heard the story told by Mr. Atkins at the club,

---

* Small catering facilities (similar to a tearoom) attached to railway stations, utilized before trains introduced in-travel dining cars.

and now Mr. Anderson gave them his version of what had occurred since the morning. Captain Fraser, therefore, asked them to stay to dinner. He said, "I am very sorry I am late, but it could not be helped. When returning from the club my horse was alarmed at something. The coachman lost control and there was almost a disaster. But, thank God, nobody is seriously hurt."

Their carriage had, however, been so badly damaged that they had to get a hackney carriage to bring them home.

In India, specially in June, they are not particular about the dress. So Captain Fraser said they would sit down to dinner at once and at a quarter after nine they all went in to dine. The Khansama who knew that something had gone wrong with Anderson Saheb stared at the uninvited guests with astonishment.

The soup was the first thing brought in and the trouble began as soon as it came. Captain Fraser's Khansama was an old hand at his business, but somehow he made a mess of things. He got so nervous about what he himself could not explain that he upset a full plate of soup that he had brought for Mr. Anderson not exactly on his head, but on his left ear.

Well the reader would understand the situation. There was a plateful of hot soup on Mr. Anderson's left ear. The soup should have got cold, because it had waited long for the Captain's return from the club, but the cook had very prudently warmed it up again and it had become very warm indeed. Mr. Anderson shouted and the Khansama let go the plate. It fell on the table in front of Mr. Anderson on its edge and rolled on. Next to Mr. Anderson was Mrs. Fraser, and there was a glass of iced-water in front of her. The rolling soup plate upset the glass, and the water and the plate all came down on Mrs. Fraser, the iced-water making her wet through and through. As she was putting on a muslin gown, she had to go and change. Mrs. Anderson at this point got up and said that they would not spoil the Frasers' dinner by their presence. She added that the curse of the Indian Fakir was on them and if they stayed the Frasers too would have to go without dinner. Naturally she anticipated that some further difficulty would arise there when the next dish was brought in. The Frasers emphatically protested loudly but she dragged Mr. Anderson away. She seemed to have forgotten that she had had her lunch, but her husband had not had any.

While going in their motor car from Mr. Fraser's house to their own they had to pass a *bazaar** on the way; and in that *bazaar* there was a

---

* Marketplace of multiple stalls.

sweetmeat shop. Mr. Anderson, whose helpless condition could be very easily imagined, ordered his chauffeur to stop at the sweetmeat shop. It was a native shop with a fat native proprietor sitting without any covering upon his body on a low stool. As soon as he saw Mr. Anderson and his wife he rushed out of his shop with joined palms to enquire what the gentleman wanted. Mr. Anderson was evidently very popular with the native tradesmen and shop keepers.

This shop keeper had special reason to know Mr. Anderson, as it was the latter's custom to give a bean-feast dinner to all his native workmen on Her Majesty's birthday, and this particular sweetmeat vendor used to get the contract for the catering. The birthday used to be observed in India on the 24th May and it was hardly a fortnight that this man had received a cheque for a pretty large amount from Mr. Anderson, for having supplied Mr. Anderson's native workmen with sweets.

Naturally he rushed out of his shop in that humble attitude. But in doing so he upset a whole dishful of sweets, and the big dish with the sweets went into the road-side drain. All the same, the man came up and wanted to know the pleasure of the Saheb. Mr. Anderson told him that he was very hungry and wanted something to eat. "Certainly, *Huzoor*," said the *Halwâi* (Indian Confectioner) and fussily rushed in. He brought out some native sweets in a "*dona*" (cup made of leaves) but as ill luck would have it Mr. Anderson could not eat anything.

There was any amount of petroleum in the sweets. How it got in there was a mystery. Mr. Anderson however asked his chauffeur to proceed. For fear of hurting the feelings of this kind old *Halwâi*, Mr. Anderson did not do anything then; but scarcely had the car gone two hundred yards when the "*dona*" with its contents untouched was on the road.

Mr. Anderson reached home at about half past ten, and he expected to find no dinner at home. But he was relieved to hear from his bearer (butler and valet combined) that dinner was ready. He rushed into the bath-room, had a cold bath and within five minutes was ready for dinner in the dining-room.

But the dinner would not come. After waiting for about fifteen minutes the bearer was dispatched to the kitchen to enquire what the matter was. The cook came with a sad look upon his face and informed him that the dinner had been ready since 8.30 as usual, but as the Saheb had not returned he had kept the food in the kitchen and come out leaving the kitchen-door open. Unfortunately the dogs had finished the dinner in his absence, probably thinking that the master was dining out. In a case like this the cook, who had been in Mr. Anderson's service for a long time, expected to hear some hard words; but Mr. Anderson only laughed loud and long. The cook suggested that he should prepare another dinner, but Mr. Anderson said that it would not be necessary that night. The chauffeur subsequently informed the cook that the master and his wife had dined at Captain Fraser's, and finished with sweets at Gopal Halwâi's shop. This explained the master's mirth to the cook's satisfaction.

What happened the next day to Mr. Anderson need not be told. It is too painful and too dirty a story. The fact remains that Mr. Anderson had no solid food the next day either, and he feared he might die of starvation, as he did not know how much longer the curse was going to last, or what else was in store for him.

On the morning of the third day the bearer reported that a certain Indian Fakir had invited Mr. Anderson to come and breakfast with him. How eagerly husband and wife went! This Fakir lived in a miserable hut on the bank of the river; and he ushered the couple in at once and gave them bread and water. Here was clean healthy looking bread after all, and Mr. Anderson never counted how many loaves he ate. But he had never eaten food with greater relish and pleasure in his life before. After the meal the Fakir who evidently knew Mr. Anderson said: "Saheb, you are a great man and a good man too. You are rich and you think that riches can purchase everything. You are wrong. The Giver of all things may turn gold into dust and gold may, by His order, lose all its purchasing power. This you have seen during the last two days. You have annoyed a man who has no gold but who has power. You think that the Deputy Commissioner has power—but he has not. The Deputy Commissioner gets his power from the King. The man whom you have offended got his power from the King of Kings.

"It is His pleasure that you should leave the station. The sooner you leave this place, Saheb, the better for you, or you will starve. You can stay as long as you like here—but you will get no food to eat outside this hut of mine—you can try.

"You may go now and come back for your dinner when you require it—."

Mr. Anderson came back to the Fakir's cottage for his dinner, with his wife at nine in the evening.

Early the next morning, he left the station and never came back.

Within a month he left India for good. The hospitable gentlemen of the station who had asked Mr. and Mrs. Anderson to have a meal with them will never forget the occasion.

This story, though it reads like a fairy tale, is nevertheless true.

All the European residents of J——knew it and if anyone of them happens to read these pages he will be able to certify that every detail is correct.

In this connection it will not be out of place to mention some of the strange doings of the once famous Hasan Khan[*], the black artist of Calcutta. Fifty years ago there was not an adult in Calcutta who did not know his name and had not seen or at least heard of his marvellous feats.

I have heard any number of wonderful stories but I shall mention only two here which, though evidently not free from exaggeration, will give an idea of what the people came to regard him as capable of achieving, and also of the powers and attributes which he used to arrogate to himself.

What happened was this.

There was a big reception in Government House at Calcutta.[†] Now every resident of the Metropolis of those days know what such a reception meant.

All public roads within half a mile of Government House were closed to wheeled and fast traffic.

The large compound was decorated with lamps and Chinese Lanterns in a manner that beggared all description. Thousands of these Chinese Lanterns hung from the trees and twinkled among the foliage like so many coloured fire-flies. The drives from the gates to the building had rows of these coloured lanterns on both sides; besides, there were coloured flags and Union Jacks flying from the tops of the poles, which had wreaths of flowers coiled round them, and which served to support the ropes or wires from which these lanterns were suspended.

The main building itself was illuminated with hundreds of thousands of candles or lamps and looked from a distance like a house on fire. From close quarters you could read "Long live the Queen" written in letters of fire on the parapets of the building, and could see the procession of carriages that passed up and down the drives so artistically decorated, and wonder that the spirited horses did not bolt or shy or kick over the traces when entering those lanes of fire.

---

[*] Fictious character.
[†] 90-room mansion and official residence of the Viceroy of India during British rule (now official residence of the Governor of West Bengal).

There were no electric lights then in Calcutta or in any part of India, no motor cars and no rubber-tyred carriages. Now-a-days Government House is illuminated by electricity; but I am told by my elders that in those days when tallow candles and tiny glass lamps were the only means of illumination the thing looked more beautiful and gorgeous. Naturally on such a night lots of people come to witness and admire the decorations of Government House.

But the people who come to see the illumination pass along the road and are not allowed to stop. The law is that they must walk on and if a young child stops for more than half a minute his guardian, friend, nurse or companion is at once reminded by the policeman on duty that he or she must walk on; and these policemen of Calcutta, unlike the policemen of London, are not at all courteous in their manner or speech.

So it happened that on a certain reception night Hasan Khan, the black artist, went to see the decorations and while lingering on the road was rudely told by the policeman on duty to get away.

Ordinarily Hasan Khan was a man of placid disposition and polite manners. He told the policeman that he should not have been rude to a rate payer* who had only come to enjoy the glorious sight and meant no harm. He also dropped a hint that if the head of the police department knew that a subordinate of his was insulting Hasan Khan it would go hard with that subordinate.

This infuriated the policeman who blew his whistle which had the effect of making half a dozen other constables appear on the scene. They then gave poor Hasan Khan a thrashing and reported him to the Inspector on duty. As chance would have it this Inspector had not heard of Hasan Khan before. So he ordered that he should be detained in custody and charged next morning with having assaulted a public officer in the discharge of his duty.

The Inspector also received a warning but he did not listen to it. Then Hasan Khan took out a piece of paper and a pencil from his pocket and wrote down the number of each of the six or seven policemen who had taken part in beating him; and he assured everybody present (a large number of persons had gathered now) that the constables and the Inspector would be dismissed from Government service within the next one hour.

Most of the people had not seen him before and, not knowing who he was, laughed. The Inspector and the constables laughed too. After the mirth

---

* Tax payer.

had subsided Hasan Khan was ordered to be handcuffed and removed. When the handcuffs had been clapped on he smiled serenely and said, "I order that all the lights within half a mile of where we are standing be put out at once." Within a couple of seconds the whole place was in utter darkness.

The entire Government House compound which was a mass of fire only a minute before was in total darkness and the street lamps had gone out too. The only light that remained was on the street lamp-post under which our friends were.

The commotion at the reception could be more easily imagined than described.

There was total darkness everywhere. The guests were treading literally on one another's toes and the accidents that happened to the carriages and horses were innumerable.

As good luck would have it another Police Inspector who was also on duty and was on horseback came up to the only light within a circle of half a mile radius.

To him Hasan Khan said, "Go and tell your Commissioner of Police that his subordinates have ill-treated Hasan Khan and tell him that I order him too to come here at once."

Some laughed, others scoffed; but the Inspector on horseback went and within ten minutes the Commissioner of the Calcutta Police came along with half a dozen other high officials enquiring what the trouble was about.

To them Hasan Khan told the story of the thrashing he had received and pointed out the assailants. He then told the Commissioner that if those constables and the Inspector who had ordered him to be handcuffed were dismissed, on the spot, from Government service, the lamps would be lighted without human assistance. To the utter surprise of everybody present (including the high officials who had come out with the Commissioner of Police) an order dismissing the constables and the Inspector was passed there and then and signed by the Commissioner in the dim light shed by that isolated lamp; and within one second of the order the entire compound of Government House was lighted up again, as if some one had switched on a thousand electric lamps controlled by a single button.

Everybody who was present there enjoyed the whole thing excessively, with the exception of the police officers who had been so summarily dismissed from service.

It appeared that the Commissioner of Police knew a lot about Hasan Khan and his black art. How he had come to know of Hasan Khan's powers will now be related.

Most of my readers have heard the name of Messrs. Hamilton and Co., Jewellers of Calcutta*. They are the oldest and most respectable firm of Jewellers probably in the whole of India.

One day Hasan Khan walked into their shop and asked to see some rings. He was shown a number of rings but he particularly approved a cheap ring set with a single ruby. The price demanded for this ring was too much for poor honest Hasan Khan's purse, so he proposed that the Jewellers should let him have the ring on loan for a month.

This, of course, the Jewellers refused to do and in a most un-Englishman-like and unbusiness-like manner a young shop assistant asked him to clear out.

He promptly walked out of the shop promising to come again the next day. Before going out of the shop, however, he told one of the managers that the young shop assistant had been very rude to him and would not let him have the ring for a month.

The next day there was a slight commotion in Hamilton's shop. The ring was missing. Of course, nobody could suspect Hasan Khan because the ring had been seen by everybody in the shop after his departure. The police were communicated with and were soon on the spot. They were examining the room and the locks and recording statements when Hasan Khan walked in with the missing ring on his finger.

He was at once arrested, charged with theft and taken to the police station and locked up.

At about midday he was produced before the Magistrate. When he appeared in court he was found wearing ten rings, one on each finger. He was remanded and taken back to his cell in the jail.

The next morning when the door of his cell was opened it was found that one of the big *almirahs†*, in which some gold and silver articles were kept in Hamilton's shop, was standing in his cell. Everybody gazed at it dumbfounded. The *almirah* with its contents must have weighed

---

* Hamilton & Co. (in operation 1808–1973): "Probably the best known and celebrated British silversmith operating in India."—*The Makers of Indian Colonial Silver 1760–1860*, by Wynyard R. T. Wilkinson (1987).

† Type of standing closet or cabinet.

fifty stones˙. How it got into the cell was beyond comprehension and was, to all appearance, a downright miracle.

Some of the big officers of Government came to see the fun and asked Hasan Khan how he had managed it.

"How did you manage to get the show-case in your drawing-room?" inquired Hasan Khan of each officer in reply to the question.

And everybody thought that the fellow was mad. But as each officer reached home he found that one show-case (evidently from Hamilton's shop) with all its contents was standing in his drawing-room.

The next morning Hasan Khan gave out in clear terms that unless Messrs. Hamilton and Co. withdrew the charge against him at once they would find their safe in which were kept the extra valuable articles, at the bottom of the Bay of Bengal.

The Jewellers, like the redoubtable knight in the play[†], were evidently of opinion that the better part of valour was discretion. The case against Hasan Khan was accordingly withdrawn and he was honourably acquitted of all charges and set at liberty.

Then rose the big question of compensating him for the incarceration he had suffered; and the ring with the single ruby, which he had fancied so much and which had caused all this trouble, was presented to him.

Of course, Messrs. Hamilton and Co., the Jewellers, had to spend a lot of money in carting back the show-cases that had so mysteriously walked away from their shop, but they were not sorry, because they could not have advertised their precious wares better, and everybody was anxious to possess something or other from among the contents of these peculiar show-cases.

It was in connection with this case that Hasan Khan became known to most of the European Government officials of Calcutta at that time.[‡]

˙ 700 pounds.

† Sir John Falstaff in *Henry IV, Part I* by William Shakespeare (Act 5, Scene 3): "The better part of valour is discretion."

‡ [Author's note: *(added to the 1921 4th edition—ed.)*] Since the above account was printed I have been informed that the Jewellers referred to therein were a different firm.

Indian Mughal-style painting *Padshahnama plate 10* by Bichitr (1628).

THE BRIDAL PARTY.

IN Benares, the sacred city of the Hindus, situated in the United Provinces of Agra and Oudh[*], there is a house which is famed pretty far and wide. It is said that the house is haunted and that no human being can pass a night in that house.

Once there was a large Bridal party.

In India the custom is that the Bridegroom goes to the house of the bride with great pomp and show with a number of friends and followers, and the ceremony of "*Kanya Dan*" (giving away the girl) takes place at the bride's house.

The number of the people who go with the bridegroom depends largely upon the means of the bride's party, because the guests who come with the groom are to be fed and entertained in right regal style. It is this feeding and entertaining the guests that makes a daughter's marriage so costly in India, to a certain extent.

If the bride and the bridegroom live in the same town or village then the bridegroom's party goes to the bride's house in the evening, the marriage is performed at night and the guests come away the same night or early the next morning. But even in such a case the guests are sometimes entertained for two or three days by the bride's guardian. If, however, the places of residence of the bride and the bridegroom are, say, three hundred miles apart as is generally the case, the bridegroom with his party goes a day or two earlier and stays a day or two after the marriage. The bride's people have to find accommodation, food and entertainment for the whole period, which in the case of rich people extends over a week.

Now I had the pleasure of joining such a bridal party as mentioned last, going to Benares.

We were about thirty young men, besides a number of elderly people.

Since the young men could not be merry in the presence of their elders the bride's father, who was a very rich man, had made arrangements to put up the thirty of us in a separate house.

This house was within a few yards of the famed haunted house.

We reached Benares at about ten in the morning and it was about three in the afternoon that we were informed that the celebrated haunted house was close by. Naturally some of us decided that we should occupy that house

---

* Now Uttar Pradesh.

rather than the one in which we were. I myself was not very keen on shifting but a few others were. Our host protested but we insisted, and so the host had to give way.

The house was empty and the owner was a local gentleman, a resident of Benares.

To procure his permission and the key was the work of a few minutes, and we entered into possession of the house at about six in the evening. It was a very large house with big rooms and halls (rather poorly furnished) but some furniture was brought in from the house which we had occupied on our arrival.

There was a very big and well-ventilated hall and in this we decided to sleep. Carpet upon carpet was piled on the floor and there we decided to sleep (on the ground) in right Oriental style*. Lamps were brought and the house was lighted up.

At about 9 P.M. our dinner was announced. The Oriental dinner is conducted as follows:—

The guests all sit on the floor spread with pieces of carpets or mats of *kusha* grass†; and a big plate of metal (say 20" in diameter), or more generally a piece of plantain leaf or what is called a *pattal* (formed of some other leaves stitched together into the shape of a plate of that size), is placed in front of each guest together with some unused earthenware cups and tumblers. Then the service commences and the plates and cups are filled with dainties. Each guest ordinarily gets thrice as much as he can eat. Then the host, who does not himself sit down with the guests, folding his hands requests them to do ample justice; and thus the dinner begins. But very little is eaten in fact, and whatever is left goes to the poor; and that is probably the only consolation. Now on this particular occasion the bride's father, who was our host and who was an elderly gentleman had withdrawn, leaving two of his sons to look after us. He himself, we understood, was looking after his more elderly guests who had been lodged in a different house.

The hall in which we sat down to dine was a large one and very well lighted. Adjoining it was the hall in which our beds had been made. The sons of *mine host* with a number of others were serving. I always was rather unconventional. So I asked my fellow guests whether I could fall to, and without waiting for permission I commenced eating, a very good thing I did, as would appear hereafter.

---

* Sleeping on the floor upon precisely arranged mats, cushions, and/or carpets.
† Tufted perennial grass often used in Hindu rituals.

In about twenty minutes the serving was over and we were asked to begin. As a matter of fact I was nearly half through at that time. And then the trouble began.

With a click all the lights went out and the whole house was in total darkness.

Of course, the reader can guess what followed.

"Who has put out the lights?" shouted Jagat, who was sitting next but one to me on the left.

"The ghost," was somebody's facetious reply.

"I shall kill him if I can catch him," shouted Jagat again.

The whole place was in darkness, we could not see anything, but we could hear that Jagat was trying to get up.

Then he received what was a stunning blow on his back. We could hear the thump.

"Oh," cried out Jagat. "Who is that?"

He sat down again and gave the man on his right a blow like the one he had received. The man on the right protested. Then Jagat turned to the man on his left. The man on Jagat's left evidently resisted and Jagat had the worst of it.

Then Narain, another member of the party, gave a loud shriek.

"What is the matter with you?" asked his neighbour.

"Why did you pull my hair" demanded Narain vehemently.

"I did not pull," shouted the neighbour.

All attempts on the part of our young hosts, who were equally nonplussed, to restore order by apologies and entreaties were of no avail.

At length in the midst of this universal hubbub a servant was seen approaching with a lamp and things became somewhat quiet.

But the servant was not destined to reach the hall. He stumbled against something and fell headlong in a heap on the ground, the lamp went out, and our trouble began again, and with it, the uproar.

One of the party received a slap on the back of his head which sent his cap rolling and in his attempt to recover it he upset a glass of water that was near his right hand.

Matters went on in this fashion until—Hail holy light!—a lamp was actually brought in. The whole thing must have taken about five minutes only. But when the lamp came we found that all the dishes were quite clean.

The eatables had mysteriously disappeared.

The sons of *mine host* looked stupidly at us and we looked stupidly at them and at one another. But there it was, there was not a particle of solid food left.

We had therefore no alternative but to adjourn to the nearest confectioner's shop and eat some sweets there. That the night would not pass in peace we were sure; but nobody dared suggest that we should not pass the night in the haunted house. Once having defied the Ghost we had to stand to our guns for one night at least.

It was well after eleven o'clock at night when we came back and went to bed. We went to bed but not to sleep.

The room in which we all slept was a big one as I have said already, and there were two wall lamps in it. We lowered the lamps and—

Then the lamps went out, and we began to anticipate trouble. Our hosts had all gone home leaving us to the tender mercies of the Ghost.

Shortly afterwards we began to feel as if we were lying on a public road and horses passing along the road within a yard of us. We also imagined we could hear men passing close to us whispering. Sleeping was impossible. We all remained awake talking about different things, till a horse seemed to come very near. And thus the night passed away. At about four in the morning one of us got up and wanted to go out.

We shouted for the servant called Kallu and within a minute Kallu came with a lantern. Our fellow guest, who had got up, then walked out of the room followed by Kallu.

We could hear him going along the dining hall to the head of the stairs. Then we heard him shriek. We all rushed out. The lighted lantern was there at the head of the stairs and our fellow guest at the bottom. Kallu had vanished.

We rushed down, picked up our friend and carried him upstairs. He said that Kallu had given him a push and he had tumbled down. Fortunately he was not hurt. We called the servants and they all came, Kallu among them. He denied having come with a lantern or having pushed our friend down the stairs. The other servants corroborated his statement. They assured us that Kallu had never left the room in which they all were.

We were satisfied that this was also a ghostly trick.

At about seven in the morning when our hosts came we were glad to bid good-bye to the haunted house with our bones whole.

The funniest thing was that only those of my fellow-guests had the worst of it who had denied the existence of Ghosts. Those of us who had kept respectfully silent had not been touched.

Those who had received a blow or two averred that the blows could not have been given by invisible hands inasmuch as the blows were too substantial. But all of us were certain that it was no trick played by a human being.

The passing horses and the whispering passers-by had given us a queer creepy sensation.

In this connection may be mentioned a few haunted houses in other parts of India. There are one or two very well-known haunted houses in Calcutta.

The "Hastings House" is one of them. It is situated at Alipore in the Southern suburb of Calcutta. This is a big palatial building now owned by the Government of Bengal. At one time it was the private residence of the Governor-General of India whose name it bears[*]. At present it is used as the "State Guest House" in which the Indian Chiefs are put up when they come to pay official visits to His Excellency in Calcutta. It appears that in a lane not very far from this house was fought the celebrated duel between Warren Hastings, the first Governor-General of India and Sir Philip Francis, a Member of his Council and the reputed author of the "Letters of Junius."[†] [‡]

While living in this house Warren Hastings married Baroness Imhoff sometime during the first fortnight of August about one hundred and forty years ago. "The event was celebrated by great festivities"; and, as expected, the bride came home in a splendid equipage. It is said that this scene is re-enacted on the anniversary of the wedding by supernatural agency and a ghostly carriage duly enters the gate in the evening once every year. The clatter of hoofs and the rattle of iron-tyred wheels are distinctly heard advancing up to the portico; then there is the sound of the opening and closing of the carriage door, and lastly the carriage proceeds onwards, but it does not come out from under the porch. It vanishes mysteriously.

To-day is the 15th of August and this famous equipage must have glided in and out to the utter bewilderment of watchful eyes and ears within the last fortnight.[§] [**]

---

[*] Warren Hastings, Governor-General of India 1773–1785.

[†] August 17, 1780: Hastings wounded Francis in this duel of bitter enemies.

[‡] Collection of anonymous letters, critical of King George III, believed to have been penned by Philip Francis.

[§] [Author's note:] Since the publication of the first edition, "Hastings House" has been converted into an Indian Rugby for the benefit of the cadets of the rich families in Bengal. (*2024 addition: It is now the Institute of Education for Women through the University of Calcutta—ed.*)

[**] Another ghost tale says that the spirit of Hastings remains in the house, eternally searching for a black bureau of valuables left behind when he returned to England.

There is another well-known ghostly house in Calcutta in which the only trouble is that its windows in the first floor bedrooms open at night spontaneously.

People have slept at night for a reward in this house closing the windows with their own hands and have waked up at night shivering with cold to find all the windows open.

Once a body of soldiers went to pass a night in this house with a view to solve the mystery. They all sat in a room fully determined not to sleep but see what happened; and thus went on chatting till it was about midnight. There was a big lamp burning on a table around which they were seated. All of a sudden there was a loud click—the lamp went out and all the windows opened simultaneously. The next minute the lamp was alight again. The occupants of the room looked at their watches; it was about 1 A.M. The next night they sat up again and one of them with a revolver. At about one in the morning this particular individual pointed his revolver at one of the windows. As soon as the lamp went out this man pulled the trigger five times and there were five reports. The windows, however, opened and the lamp was alight again as on the previous night. They all rushed to the window to see if any damage had been done by the bullets.

The five bullets were found in the room but from their appearance it seemed as if they had struck nothing, evidently the bullets would have been changed in shape if they had impinged upon any hard substance. Then this was another enigma. How did the bullets come back? No man could have put the bullets there before (for they were still hot when discovered), or could have guessed the bore of the revolver that was going to be used. However, to make assurance doubly sure, these soldiers were again present in the room on the third night, but on this occasion they had loaded their revolver with marked bullets.

As it neared one o'clock, one of them pointed the revolver at the window. He had decided to pull the trigger as soon as the lamp would go out. But he could not. As soon as the lamp went out this soldier received a sharp cut on his wrist with a cane and the revolver fell clattering on the floor. The invisible hand had left its mark behind which his companions saw after the lamp was alight again.

Many people have subsequently tried to solve the mystery but never succeeded.

The house remained untenanted for a long time; finally it was rented by an Australian horse dealer who however did not venture to occupy the building itself, and contented himself with erecting his stables and offices in the compound where he is not molested by the unearthly visitors.

There is another ghostly house and it is in the Central Provinces[*]. The name of the town has been intentionally omitted. Various people had seen numerous strange things in that house; but a correct report never came, until a friend of mine once passed a night in that house. He told me what he had seen. Most marvellous! As I have no reason to disbelieve his statements I quote portions of them here almost *verbatim*.

"I went to pass a night in that house, and having provided myself a comfortable chair, a small table, a good lamp and a few magazines, besides a loaded revolver, I occupied a front room on the ground floor. I had taken care to load that revolver myself so that there might be no trick and I had given everybody to understand that.

"I began well. The night was cool and pleasant. The lamp bright—the chair comfortable—and the magazine, which I took up, interesting.

"But at about midnight I began to feel rather uneasy.

"At one in the morning I should probably have left the place if I had not been afraid of the jeers of friends whose servants I knew were watching the house and its front door.

"At half past one I heard a peculiar sigh of pain in the next room. 'This is rather interesting,' I thought. 'To face something tangible is comparatively easy; to wait for the unknown is much more difficult.' I took out the revolver from my pocket and examined it. It looked quite all right—this small piece of metal which could have killed six men in half a minute. Then I waited—for what—well.

"A couple of minutes of suspense and the sigh was repeated. I went to the door dividing the two rooms and pushed it open. A long thick ray of light at once penetrated the darkness, and I walked into the other room. It was only partially light. But after a minute I could see all the corners. There was nothing in that room.

"I waited for a minute or two. Then I heard the sigh in the room which I had left. I came back—stopped—rubbed my eyes—.

"Sitting in the chair which I had vacated not two minutes ago was a young girl calm, fair, beautiful with that painful expression on her face which could be more easily imagined than described.

---

[*] Changed in this 4th edition from "United Provinces" to "Central Provinces."

"I had heard of her, but was not prepared for the fascinating vision—for the loveliness, 'that parts not quite with parting breath.'[*] So many others who had come to pass a night in that house had seen her and given a glowing account of her charms,—and I had disbelieved.

"Well—there she sat, calm, sad, beautiful, in my chair. If I had come in five minutes later I might have found her reading the magazine which I had left open, face downwards. When I was well within the room she stood up facing me and I stopped. The revolver fell from my hand. She smiled a sad sweet smile. How beautiful she was!

"Then she spoke. A modern ghost speaking like Hamlet's father, just think of that!

"'You will probably wonder why I am here—I shall tell you, I was murdered—by my own father ... I was a young widow living in this house which belonged to my father. I became unchaste and to save his own name he poisoned me when I was *enceinte*[†]—another week and I should have become a mother; but he poisoned me and my innocent child died too—it would have been such a beautiful baby—and you would probably want to kiss it.'

"I had kept my head cool and my gaze steadfast so far. But horror of horrors! She took out the child from her womb and showed it to me. Then she began to move in my direction dandling[‡] the child in her arms and muttering—'You will like to kiss it.'

"I don't know whether I shouted out 'Angels and ministers of grace defend us'[§]—but I fainted—that is certain.

"When I recovered consciousness it was broad day light, and I was lying on the floor, with the revolver by my side. I picked it up and slowly walked out of the house with as much dignity as I could command. At the door I met one of my friends to whom I told a lie that I had seen nothing.—It is the first time that I have told any one what I saw at the place. The Ghostly woman spoke the language of the part of the country in which the Ghostly house is situate."

The friend who told me this story, being a well educated gentleman is

---

[*] "The Giaour, a Fragment of a Turkish Tale" by Lord Byron (1813).
[†] Pregnant.
[‡] Moving (as in an infant) in a playful or affectionate way.
[§] *Hamlet* by William Shakespeare (Act 1, Scene 4).

not likely to make a garbled statement. Besides what has been written above has been confirmed by others who had passed nights in that Ghostly house; but they had generally shouted for help and fainted at the sight of the ghost though so lovely; and thus they had not heard her story from her lips.

The house still exists, but it is now a dilapidated old affair, and the roof and the doors and windows are so bad that people don't care to go and pass a night there any longer.

There is also a haunted house in Assam. In this house a certain gentleman committed suicide by cutting his own throat with a razor.

You often see him sitting on a cot in the verandah heaving deep sighs.

Mention of this house has been made in a book called "Tales from the Tiger Land" published in England. The Author says he has passed a night in the house in question and testifies to the accuracy of all the rumours that are current.

Talking about haunted houses reminds me of a haunted tank[*]. I was visiting a friend of mine in the interior of Bengal during our annual summer holidays when I was yet a student. This friend of mine was the son of a rich man and in the village had a large ancestral house where his people usually resided. It was the first week of June when I reached my friend's house. I was informed that among other things of interest, which were, however, very few in that particular part of the country, there was a large *pukka* tank belonging to my friend's people which was haunted.

What kind of Ghost lived in the tank or near it nobody could say, but what everybody knew was this, that on *Jyeshtha Shukla Ekadashi*[†] (that is, on the eleventh day after the new moon in the month of Jyeshtha) that occurs about the middle of June, the Ghost comes to bathe in the tank at about midnight.

As Jyeshtha Shukla Ekadashi was only three days off, I decided to prolong my stay at my friend's place, so that I too might have a look at the Ghost's bath.

On the eventful day I resolved to pass the night with my friend and two other intrepid souls, near the tank.

After a rather late dinner, we started with a bedding and a Hookah and a pack of cards and a big lamp. We made the bed (a mattress and a sheet) on a platform on the bank. There were six steps, with risers about nine inches each, leading from the platform to the water. Thus we were about four and

---

[*] Reservoir or pool often part of, or near to, a temple complex.
[†] Corrected for spelling in this edition from *Jaistha Shukla Ekadashi*.

a half feet above the water level; and from this coign of vantage* we could command a full view of the tank, which covered an area of about four acres. Then we began our game of cards. There was a servant with us who was preparing our Hookah.

At midnight we felt we could play no longer. The strain was too great; the interest too intense.

We sat smoking and chatting and asked the servant to remove the lamp as a lot of insects was coming near attracted by the light. As a matter of fact we did not require any light because there was a brilliant moon. At one o'clock in the morning and before I could finish reciting "How sweet the moonlight sleeps upon the bank"† there was a noise as of rushing wind—we looked round and found that not a leaf was moving but still the whizzing noise as of a strong wind continued. Then we perceived something advancing towards the tank from the opposite bank. As there was a large number of cocoanut trees near the bank on the other side, we could not in the moonlight positively decide what it really was. But it looked like a huge white elephant or prehistoric mastodon. It approached the tank at a rapid pace—say, the pace of a fast trotting horse. From the bank it took a long leap and with a tremendous splash fell into the water. The plunge made the water rise on our side and it rose as high as four and a half feet because we got wet through and through.

The mattress and the sheet and all our clothes were also wet. In the confusion we forgot to keep our eyes on the Ghost or white elephant or whatever it was, and when we again looked in that direction everything was quiet. The apparition had vanished.

The most wonderful thing was the rise in the water level. For the water to rise four and a half feet would have been impossible under ordinary circumstances even if a thousand elephants had got into the water.

We were all wide awake—We went home immediately because we required a change of clothes.

The old man (my friend's father) was waiting for us. "Well you are wet," he said.

"Yes sir," said we.

"Rightly served," was the old man's caustic remark.

He did not ask what had happened. We were told subsequently that he had got drenched like us a number of times when he was a youngster himself.

---

* Favorable position for observation.
† Lorenzo in *The Merchant of Venice* by William Shakespeare (Act 5, Scene 1).

View of the "haunted" Hastings House from
Calcutta, Past and Present by Kathleen Blechynden (1905).

Miniature painting attributed to Muhammad Qasim, in the first half of the 17th century, depicts a bride throwing herself onto her husband's funeral pyre in an act of Sutteeism.

A STRANGE INCIDENT.

WHEN I was at college there happened what was a most inexplicable incident.

The matter attracted some attention at that time, but has now been forgotten as it was really not so very extraordinary. The police in fact, when called in, explained the matter or at least thought they had done so, to everybody's satisfaction. I was, however, not satisfied with the explanation given by the police. This was what actually happened.

The college was a very big one with a large boarding-house attached to it. The boarding-house was a building separate from the college situated at a distance of about one hundred yards from the college building. It was in the form of a quadrangle with a lawn in the centre. The area of this lawn must have been 2,500 square yards. Of course it was surrounded on all sides by buildings, that is, by a row of single rooms on each side.

In the boarding-house there was a common room for the amusement of the students. There were provisions for all sorts of indoor games including a miniature billiard table in this common room. I was a regular visitor there. I did not care for any other indoor game than chess, though chess meant keeping out of bed, till late at night.

On this particular occasion, I think it was in November, a certain gentleman, who was an ex-student of the college, was paying us a visit. He was staying with us in the boarding-house. He had himself passed four years in that boarding-house and naturally had a love for it. In his time he was very popular with the other boarders and with the Superintendent, Dr. M.N., an English gentleman who was also an inmate of the boarding-house. With the permission of the learned Doctor, the Superintendent, we decided to make a night of it, and so we all assembled in the common room after dinner. I can picture to myself the cheerful faces of all the students present on that occasion in the well-lighted Hall. So far as I know only one of that group is now dead. He was the most jovial and the best beloved of all. May he rest in peace!

Now to return from this mournful digression. I could see old Mathura sitting next to me with a *Hookah* with a very long stem, directing the moves of the chessmen. There was old Birju at the miniature billiard table poking with his cue at everybody who laughed when he missed an easy shot.

Then came in the Superintendent. Dr. M.N. and, in a hurry to conceal his *Hookah* (Indians never smoke in the presence of their elders and superiors), old Mathura nearly upset the table on which the chessmen were; and the mirth went on with redoubled vigour as the Doctor was one of the loudest and merriest of the whole lot on such occasions.

Thus we went on till nearly one in the morning when the Doctor ordered everyone to go to bed. Of course we were glad to retire hoping to enjoy undisturbed rest till daybreak, but we soon found that our hopes were doomed to disappointment.

Earlier in the evening we had been playing a friendly Hockey match, and one of the players, let us call him Ram Gholam, had been slightly hurt. As a matter of fact he always got hurt whenever he played.

During the evening the hurt had been forgotten but as soon as he was in bed it was found that he could not sleep. The matter was reported to the Superintendent who finding that there was really nothing the matter with him suggested that the affected parts should be washed with hot water and finally wrapped in heated leaves of the castor-oil plant and then bandaged over with flannel. (This is the best medicine for gouty pain—not for hurt caused by a hockey stick.)

Fortunately there was a castor tree in the compound and a servant was despatched to bring the leaves. In the meantime a few of us went to the kitchen, made a fire and boiled some water. While thus engaged we heard a noise and a cry for help. We rushed out and ran along the verandah (corridor) towards the place whence the cry came. It was emanating from the room of Prayag, one of the boarders. We pushed the door but found that it was bolted from inside, we shouted to him to open but he would not. The door had four glass panes on the top and we discovered that the upper bolt only had been used; as a matter of fact the lower bolts had all been removed, because on closing the door from outside, once it had been found that a bolt at the bottom had dropped into its socket and the door had to be broken before it could be opened.

Prayag's room was in darkness. There was a curtain inside and so we could see nothing from outside. We could hear Prayag groaning. The Superintendent came up at this stage. To break the glass pane nearest to the bolt was the work of a minute. The door was opened and we all rushed in. It was a room 14'x12'; many of us could not, therefore, come in. When we went in we took a light with us. It was one of the hurricane lanterns—the one we had taken to the kitchen. The lamp suddenly went out. At the same time a brickbat* came rattling down from, or rather through, the roof and fell so close to my feet that I could almost feel it and tell what it was. And Prayag groaned again. Dr. M.N. too came in, and we helped Prayag out of his bed and took him out on the verandah. Then we saw another brickbat come from the roof of the verandah and fall in front of Prayag a few inches from his feet. We took him to the central lawn and stood in the middle of it. This time a full-sized solid brick came from the sky. It fell a few inches from my feet and remained standing on its edge. If it had toppled over it would have fallen on my toes.

By this time all the boarders had come up. Prayag stood in the middle of the group shivering and sweating. A few more brickbats came but not one of us was hurt. Then the trouble ceased. We removed Prayag to the Superintendent's room and put him in the Doctor's bed. There was a reading lamp on a stool near the head of the bed and a Holy Bible on it. The learned Doctor must have been reading it when he was disturbed. Another bed was brought in and the Doctor passed the night in it.

In the morning came the police.

They found a goodly heap of brickbats and bones in Prayag's room and on the lawn. There was an investigation, but nothing came out of it. The police however explained the matter as follows:—

There were some people living in the two-storied houses in the neighbourhood. The brickbats and the bones must have come from there. As a matter of fact the police discovered that the boarding-house students and the people who lived in these houses were not on good terms. Those people had organized a music party and the students had objected to it. The matter had been reported to the Magistrate and had ended in a decision in favour of the students. Hence the strained relations. This was the most natural explanation and the only explanation. But this explanation did not satisfy me for several reasons.

The first reason was that the college compound contained another well-kept lawn that stretched between the College boarding-house and those two-storied buildings. But there were no brickbats on this lawn. If brickbats had been thrown from those buildings, some at least would have fallen upon the lawn.

Then as regarded the brickbats that were in the room, they had all dropped from the ceiling; but in the morning we found the tiles of the roof intact. Then again in the middle of the central lawn there was at least one

---

* A fragmented piece of brick, especially when used as a missile (weapon).

entire brick. But the nearest building from which a brick might have been thrown was at a distance of one hundred yards, and to throw a whole brick 9"x4½"x3" such a distance would require a machine of some kind or other and none was found in the house.

The last thing that created doubts in my mind was this, that not one brickbat had hit anybody. There were so many of us there and there was such an abundance of brickbats, still not one of us was hit. In fact, the entire brick that fell and stood on edge within three inches of my toe would have hurt me if it had only toppled over. And it is well known that brickbats hurled by Ghostly hands do not hit anybody.

Most of the readers are aware that Sutteeism was the practice of burning the widows on the funeral pyre of their dead husbands. This practice was prevalent in Bengal, and in some other parts of what was then known as the Presidency of Fort William[*], down to the year 1829 when a law (Regulation XVII of 1829) forbidding and penalizing the aiding and abetting of sutteeism was passed. Before that enactment of course, many women had in a manner been forced to become Suttees. The public opinion against a widow's surviving was so great that she preferred to die at once rather than live after her husband's death.

The law has, however, changed the custom and the public opinion too. Still, every now and then there are found cases of determined Sutteeism among all classes in India who profess Hinduism. Frequent instances are found in Bengal; and whenever a case comes to the notice of the public the newspapers report it in a manner which shows that respect for the Suttee is not yet dead. Sometimes a verdict of "Suicide during temporary insanity" is returned, but, of course, whoever reads the report can not fail to grasp how matters stand.

I know of a recent case in which a gentleman who was in Government service died leaving a young widow.

When the husband's dead body was being removed the wife did not look particularly aggrieved, and nobody suspected that anything was wrong with her.

But when all the members of the family had gone away with the bier[†]

---

[*] Largest of three provincial governments (administrative divisions) of India, the other two being the Presidency of Fort St. George and the Presidency of Bombay.
[†] Frame on which a coffin is carried.

the young widow quietly procured a tin of Kerosine oil and a few bed sheets. She soaked the bed sheets well in the oil and then wrapped them tightly round her person and further secured them by means of a rope. She then shut all the doors of her room and set the clothes on fire. By the time the doors were forced open (there were only ladies in the house at that time) she was dead.

Of course this was a case of suicide pure and simple and there was the usual verdict of suicide during temporary insanity, but I personally doubt the insanity very much, there being so much method in it.

The one that I am now going to relate is more interesting and more mysterious, and probably more instructive.

Babu Bhagwan Prasad, now the late Babu Bhagwan Prasad, was a clerk in the——office in the United Provinces. He was a middle-aged man of forty-five when the incident happened.

He had an attack of cold which subsequently developed into pneumonia and after a lingering illness of eight days he died at about eight o'clock one morning.

He had, as expected, a wife and a number of children. Besides as a well-paid officer, he maintained a large family consisting of brothers—their wives and their children.

At the time of his death, in fact, when the doctor went away in the morning giving his verdict that it was a question of minutes, his wife seemed the least affected of all. While all the members of the family were collected round the bed of their dying relative the lady withdrew to her room saying that she was going to dress for the journey. Nobody took any serious notice of her at the time. She retired to her room and dressed herself in the most elaborate style, and marked her forehead with a large quantity of "*Sindur*"* for the last time.

After dressing she came back to the room where her dying husband was and approached the bed. Those who were there made way for her in surprise. She sat down on the bed and finally lay down by her dying husband's side. This demonstration of sentimentalism could not be tolerated in a family where the *Purda* is strictly observed and one or two elderly ladies tried to remonstrate. But on touching her they found that she was dead. The husband was dead too. They had both died simultaneously. When the doctor arrived he found the lady dead, but he could not ascertain the cause of her death.

---

* [Author's note:] "Sindur" is red oxide of mercury or lead used by orthodox Hindu women in some parts of India whose husbands are alive; widows do not use it.

Everybody thought she had taken poison but nothing could be discovered by *post mortem* examination. There was not a trace of any kind of poison in the body.

The funeral of the husband and the wife took place that afternoon and they were cremated on the same pyre.

The stomach and some portions of the intestines of the deceased lady were sent to the chemical examiner and his report (which arrived a week later) did not disclose anything.

The matter remains a mystery.

It will never be found out what force killed the lady at such a critical moment. Probably it was the strong will of the Suttee that would not allow her body to be separated from that of her husband even in death.

Another very strange incident is reported from a place near Agra, in the United Provinces.

There were two respectable residents of the town who were close neighbours. For the convenience of the readers we shall call them Smith and Jones.

Smith and Jones were not only, as has already been said, close neighbours but they were also the best of friends. Each had his wife and children living with him.

Unfortunately Smith got fever, on a certain very hot day in June. The fever would not leave him, and on the tenth day it was declared to be a case of typhoid fever of the worst type.

Now typhoid fever is in itself very dangerous, but more so in the case of a person who gets it in June. So poor Smith had no chance of recovery. Of course Jones knew it. Mrs. Smith was a rather uneducated elderly lady and the children were too young. So the medical treatment as well as the general management of Smith's affairs was left entirely in the hands of Jones.

Jones did his best. He procured the best medical advice. He got the best medicines prescribed by the doctors and engaged the best nurse available. But his efforts were of no avail. On a certain Thursday afternoon Smith began to sink fast and at about eight in the evening he died.

Jones on his return from his office that day at about four in the afternoon had been informed that Smith's condition was very bad, and he had at once gone over to see what he could do.

He had called in half a dozen doctors, but they had all pronounced the case hopeless. Three of the doctors had accordingly gone away, but the other three had stayed behind.

When however Smith was dead, and these three doctors had satisfied themselves that life was quite extinct, they too went away with Jones leaving the dead body in charge of the mourning members of the family of the deceased.

Jones at once set about making arrangements for the funeral early the next morning; and it was well after eleven at night that he returned to a very late dinner at his own house. It was a particularly hot night and after smoking his last cigar for the day Jones went to bed, but not to sleep, after midnight. The death of his old friend and neighbour had made him very sad and thoughtful. The bed had been made on the open roof on the top of the house which was a two storied building and Jones lay watching the stars and thinking.

At about one in the morning there was a loud knock at the front door. Jones who was wide awake thought it was one of the servants returning home late and so he did not take any notice of it.

After a few moments the knock was repeated at the door which opened on the stairs leading to the roof of the second storey on which Jones was sleeping. [The visitor had evidently passed through the front door]. This time Jones knew it was no servant. His first impression was that it was one of the mutual friends who having heard of Smith's death was coming to make enquiries. So he shouted out, "Who is there?"

"It is I,—Smith," was the reply.

"Smith—Smith is dead," stammered Jones.

"I want to speak to you, Jones—open the door or I'll come and kill you," said the voice of Smith from beyond the door below. A cold sweat stood on Jones's forehead. It was Smith speaking, there was no doubt of that,— Smith, whom he had seen expire before his very eyes five hours ago. Jones began to look for a weapon to defend himself.

There was nothing available except a rather heavy hammer which had been brought up an hour earlier that very night to fix a nail in the wall for hanging a lamp. Jones took this up and waited for the spirit of Smith at the head of the stairs.

The spirit passed through this closed door also. Though the staircase was in total darkness still Jones could see Smith coming up step by step. Up and up came Smith and breathlessly Jones waited with the hammer in his hand. Now only three steps divided them.

"I shall kill you," hissed Smith. But Jones aimed a blow with the hammer and hit Smith between the eyes. With a groan Smith fell down. Jones also fainted.

A couple of hours later there was a great commotion at the house of Smith. The dead body had mysteriously disappeared.

The first thing they could think of was to go and inform Jones.

So one of the young sons of Smith came to Jones's house. The servant admitted him and told him where to find the master.

Young Smith knocked at the door leading to the staircase but got no reply. "After his watchful night, he is sleeping soundly," thought young Smith.

But then Jones must be awakened.

The whole household woke up but not Jones. One of the servants then procured a ladder and got upon the roof. Jones was not upon his bed nor under it either. The servant thought he should open the door leading to the staircase and admit the people who were standing outside beyond the door at the bottom of the stairs. There was a number of persons now at the door including Mrs. Jones, her children, and servants, and young Smith.

But the servant stumbled over something and though it was dark he knew it was the body of his master. He, however, passed on and then stumbled again. There was another human being in the way. "Who is this other?—probably a thief," thought the servant.

At last he reached the door and opening it admitted the people who were outside. They had lights with them, and as they came up, it was found that the second body on the stairs two or three steps below the landing was the dead body of Smith while the body on the landing was the unconscious form of Jones.

Restoratives were applied and Jones came to his senses and then related the story that has been recorded above. A doctor was summoned and he found the wound caused by Jones's hammer on Smith's head. There was a deep cut but no blood had come out, therefore, it appeared that the wound must have been caused at least two or three hours after death.

The doctors never investigated whether death could have been caused by the blow given by the hammer. They thought there was no need of an investigation either, because they had left Smith quite dead at eight in the evening.

How Smith's dead body was spirited away and came to Jones's house has been a mystery which will probably never be solved.

Thinking over the matter recorded above the writer has come to the conclusion that probably a natural explanation might be given of the affair.

Taking however all the facts of the case as given above to be true (and there is no reason to suppose that they are not) the only explanation that could be given and in fact that was given by some of the sceptical minds of Agra at that time was as follows:—

"Smith was dead. Jones was a very old friend of his. He was rather seriously affected. He must have, in an unconscious state of mind like a somnambulist, carried the dead body of Smith to his own house without being detected in the act. Then his own fevered imagination endowed Smith with the faculty of speech, dead though the latter was; and in a moment of—well—call it temporary insanity, if you please—he inflicted the wound on the forehead of Smith's dead body."

This was the only plausible explanation that could be given of the affair; but regard being had to the fact that Smith's dead body was lying in an upper storey of the house and that there was a number of servants between the death chamber and the main entrance to the house, the act of removing the dead body without their knowing it was a difficult task, nay utterly impracticable.

Over and above this it was not feasible to carry away even at night, the dead body along the road, which is a well frequented thoroughfare, without being observed by anybody.

Then there is the third fact that Jones was really not such a strong person that he could carry unaided Smith's body that distance with ease.

Smith's dead body as recovered in Jones' house had bare feet; whether there was any dust on the feet, had not been observed by anybody; otherwise some light might have been thrown on this apparently miraculous incident.

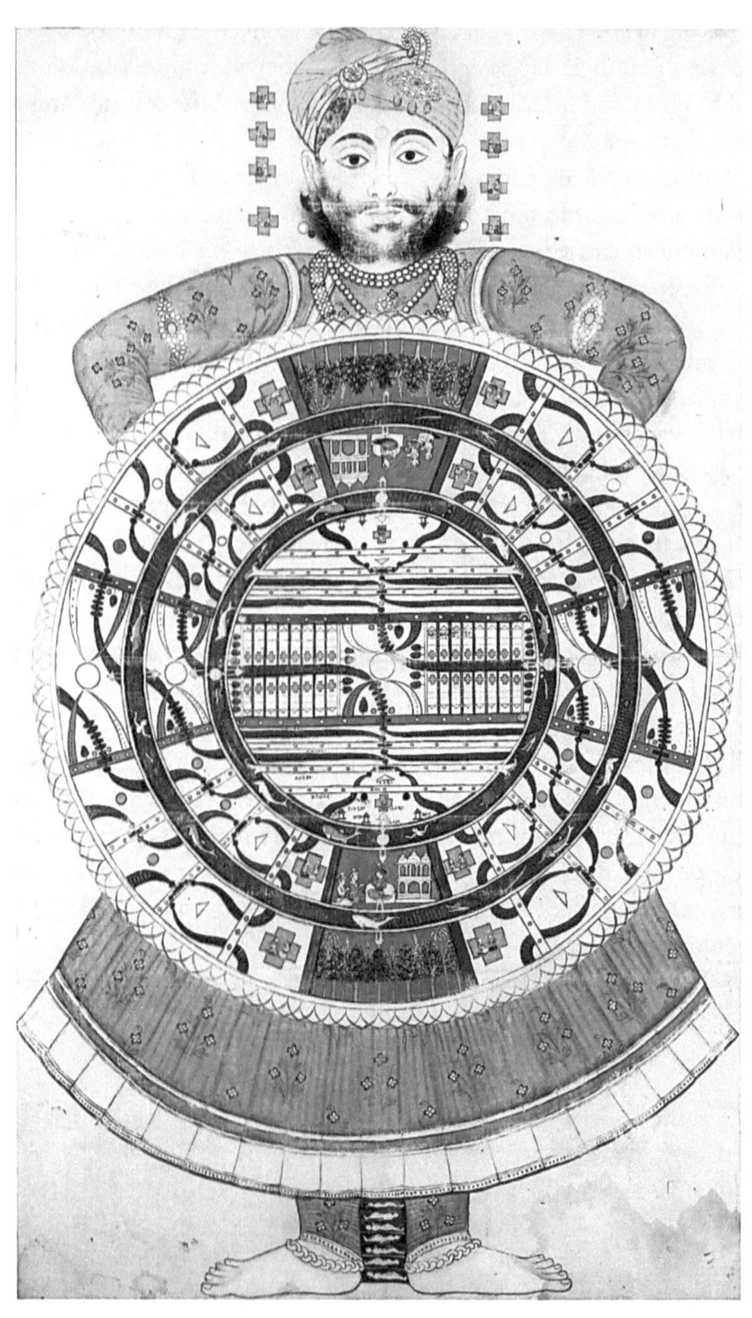

Uncredited painting of the Cosmic Purusha
(creation myth relating to life and death), 19ᵗʰ century, India.

WHAT THE PROFESSOR SAW.

THIS story is not so painful as the one entitled "What Uncle Saw." How we wish that uncle had seen something else, but all the same how glad we are that uncle did not see what the professor saw. The professor is an M.A. of the University of Calcutta, in Chemistry, and is a Lecturer in a big college. This, of course, I only mention to show that this is not the invention of a foolish person.

I shall now tell the story as I heard it from the professor.

"I was a professor of chemistry in a Calcutta college in the year 18——. One morning I received a letter from home informing me that my eldest brother was ill. It was a case of fever due to cold. Of course, a man does sometimes catch cold and get fever too. There was nothing extraordinary about that.

"In the evening I did not receive any further news. This meant that my brother was better, because in any other case they would have written.

"A number of friends came to my diggings* in the evening and invited me to join their party then going to a theatre. They had reserved some seat but one of the party for whom a seat had been reserved was unavoidably detained and hence a vacant seat. The news of my brother's illness had made me a little sad; the theatre, I thought, would cheer me up. So I joined.

"We left the theatre at about one in the morning. As I was returning home along the now deserted but well-lighted "College Street" of Calcutta I saw from a distance a tall man walking to and fro on the pavement in front of the Senate Hall. When I approached nearer I found that it was my brother of whose illness I had heard in the morning. I was surprised.

"'What are you doing here—brother,' I asked.

"'I came to tell you something.'

"'But you were ill—I heard this morning—By what train did you come?' I inquired.

"'I did not come by train—never mind—I went to your *"Basa"* (lodgings) and found you were out—gone to the theatre, so I waited for you here as I thought you would prefer walking home to driving in a hackney carriage—'

"'Very fortunate I did not take one—'

---

* Lodging for students.

"'In that case I would have seen you at your quarters.'

"'Then come along with me—' I said.

"'No,' he replied. 'I shall stay where I am—what I have come to tell you is this, that after I am gone you will take care of the mother* and see that she has everything she wants—'

"'But where are you going—' I asked puzzled.

"'Never mind where I am going—but will you promise—'

"'Promise what—?' I asked.

"'That you will see that the mother has everything and she wants for nothing.'

"'Certainly—but where on earth are you going—' I asked again.

"'I can depend upon your promise then,' he said and vanished.

"He vanished mysteriously. In what direction he went I could not say. There was no bye-lane near. It was a very well-lighted part of the city. He evidently vanished into thin air. I rubbed my eyes and looked round.

"A policeman was coming along. He was about fifty feet away.

"I inquired if he had seen the gentleman who was talking to me.

"'Did you see the other gentleman, officer?' I asked.

"'Yes,' he said looking around, 'there were two of you—where is the other—has he robbed you of all you had—these pickpockets have a mysterious way of disappearing—'

"'He was my brother,' I said, 'and no pickpocket.'

"The policeman looked puzzled too.

"I shouted aloud calling my brother by his name but received no reply. I took out my gold watch. It was half past one. I walked home at a brisk pace.

"At home I was informed by the servant that my brother had come to look for me an hour earlier, but on being told that I was out, had gone away.

"Whenever he came to Calcutta from the suburbs he put up with a friend of his instead of with me. So I decided to look him up at his friend's house in the morning. But I was not to be, Providence having ordained otherwise.

"Early the next morning I received a telegram that my brother was dead. The telegram had been sent at 1.20 A.M. He must have died an hour before. Well—there it was.

"I had seen him and so had the policeman. The servants had seen him too. There could be no mistake about that.

"I took an early train and reached my suburban home at 10 A.M. I was

---

* Presumably meaning "our" mother.

informed that my brother had died at midnight. But I had seen him at about half past one and the servant had seen him at about 12.30. I did not tell anybody anything at that time. But I did so afterwards. I was certainly not dreaming—because the conversation we had was a pretty long one. The servant and the police constable could not have been mistaken either. But the mystery remains."

This was the exact story of the professor. Here is something else to the point.

Suicidal Telepathy.

A remarkable case of what may be called suicidal telepathy has occurred near Geneva. Mme. Simon, a Swiss widow aged fifty, had been greatly distressed on account of the removal of her sister, who was five years younger, to a hospital. On Monday afternoon a number of persons who had ascended the Saleve, 4,299 feet high, by the funicular railway, were horrified to see a woman walk out on to a ledge overlooking a sheer precipice of three hundred feet, and, after carefully wrapping a shawl round her head and face, jump into space. The woman was Mme. Simon, says the *Times of India*, and she was found on the cliffs below in a mangled condition.

At the same time Mme. Simon's sister, who had not seen or communicated with the former for a week, became hysterical saying her sister was dead and that she did not want to survive her. During the temporary absence of the nurse the woman got out of her bed—opened the window and jumped into the road from the first floor. She is seriously injured and her recovery is doubtful.

The news of the death of Mme. Simon was only known at the hospital nine hours later.—*The Leader—Allahabad, 12th February, 1913.*

Much more wonderful than all this is the story of "The Astral Lady" which appeared in one of the English Magazines a few months ago. In that case an English medical gentleman saw the *Astral Lady* in a first class railway compartment in England. Only accidentally he afterwards discovered the body of a lady nearly murdered and concealed under one of the seats. His medical help and artificial respiration and stimulants brought her round, and then the doctor saw the original of the Astral Lady in the recovered girl. Well—well—wonderful things do happen sometimes.

The phenomenon mentioned in this chapter as *the professor's experience* is not at all unique. Mr. Justice Norman[*] of the Calcutta High Court is said to have seen his mother while sitting in court one day and others saw her

---

[*] Sir John Paxton Norman (1819–1871).

too. A few hours later his Lordship received a telegram informing him of her death at the very moment when he had seen her in court. This was in broad daylight; and unlike the professor, the judge did not even know that his mother was ill. But the peculiarity of the Professor's case is that the ghost not only appeared in human shape but actually discussed family affairs like a living person.

The fact that immediately after death the dead person appears to some one near and dear to him has also been vouched for by others whose veracity and intelligence cannot be questioned.

The appearance of Miss Orme[*] after her death at Mussoorie to Miss Mountstephen[†] in Lucknow was related in the Allahabad High Court during the trial of the latter lady for the murder of the former. This is on the record of the case. This case created a good deal of interest at the time.

Similar to what has been described above is the experience of Lord Brougham[‡].

An extract from his memoirs[§] is as follows:—"A most remarkable thing happened to me. So remarkable that I must tell the story from the beginning. After I left the High School (*i.e.* Edinburgh) I went with G—— my most intimate friend, to attend the classes of the University.

"There was no divinity class, but we frequently in our walks discussed many grave subjects—among others—*the Immortality of the soul and a future state.* This question and the possibility of the dead appearing to the living were subjects of much speculation, and we actually committed the folly of drawing up an agreement, written with our blood, to the effect that whichever of us died the first should appear to the other and thus solve the doubts we had entertained of the life after death.

"After we had finished our classes at the college, G——went to India having got an appointment in the Civil Service there. He seldom wrote to me and after the lapse of a few years, I had nearly forgotten his existence. One

---

[*] Frances Garnett-Orme, who was murdered in 1911 (in Lucknow) by poisoning. Her murder later inspired Agatha Christie's first novel *The Mysterious Affair at Styles.*

[†] Corrected to Mountstephen from "Mounce-Stephen"; Eva Mountstephen, travelling companion to Frances Garnett-Orme, was suspected of the murder but never found guilty.

[‡] Henry Peter Brougham (1778–1868), 1st Baron Brougham; Lord High Chancellor of Great Britain (1830–1834).

[§] *The Life and Times of Henry Lord Brougham: Written by Himself,* published posthumously in 1871.

day I had taken a warm bath, and, while lying in it enjoying the heat, I turned my head round, looking towards the chair on which I had deposited my clothes, as I was about to get out of the bath. On the chair sat G——looking calmly at me. How I got out of the bath I know not, but on recovering my senses I found myself sprawling on the floor. The apparition or whatever it was that had taken the likeness of G——had disappeared. The vision had produced such a shock that I had no inclination to talk about it or to speak about it even to Stuart*, but the impression it made upon me was too vivid to be forgotten easily, and so strongly was I affected by it that I have here written down the whole history with the date, 19th December, and all particulars as they are fresh before me now. No doubt I had fallen asleep and that the appearance presented so distinctly before my eyes was a dream I cannot doubt, yet for years I had no communication with G——nor had there been anything to recall him to my recollection. Nothing had taken place concerning our Swedish travel connected with G——or with India or with anything relating to him or to any member of his family. I recollected quickly enough our old discussion and the bargain we had made. I could not discharge from my mind the impression that G——must have died and his appearance to me was to be received by me as a proof of a future state."

This was on the 19th December, 1799.

In October 1862 Lord Brougham added a postscript.

"I have just been copying out from my Journal the account of this strange dream.

"*Certissima mortis imago!*† And now to finish the story begun about sixty years ago: Soon after my return to Edinburgh there arrived a letter from India announcing G's death, and that he died on the 19th December, 1799."—*The Pall Mall Magazine* (1914) pp. 183–184.

Another very fine story and one to the point comes from Hyderabad.

A certain Mr. J——who was an Englishman, after reading the memoirs of Lord Brougham, was so affected that he related the whole story to his confidential Indian servant. We need not mention here what Mr. J's profession was, all that we need say is that he was not very rich and in his

----

* Corrected from Stewart to "Stuart," per Lord Brougham's original writing, this referencing Charles Stuart, 1st Baron Stuart de Rothesay, whom Lord Brougham named as his "most intimate friend."

† Latin: "*A certain image of death!*"

profession there was no chance of his getting up one morning to find himself a millionaire.

The master and servant executed a bond written with their blood that he who died first would see the other a rich man.

As it happened the native servant died first, and on his death Mr. J——who was then a young man retired altogether from his business, which business was not in a very flourishing condition. Within a couple of years he went to England a millionaire. How he came by his money remains a secret. People in England were told that he had earned it in India. He must have done so, but the process of his earning he has kept strictly to himself. Mr. J——is still alive and quite hale.

A different event in which another friend of mine was concerned was thus described the other day. He had received a telegram to the effect that a very near relation of his was dying in Calcutta and that this dying person was desirous to see him. He started for Calcutta in all haste by the mail. The mail used to leave his station at about 3 P.M. in the afternoon and reach Calcutta early the next morning. It was hot weather and in his first class compartment there was no other passenger. He lay down on one of the sleeping berths and the other one was empty. All the lamps including the night light had been switched off and the compartment would have been in total darkness, but for the moonlight. The moon beams too did not come into the compartment itself as the moon was nearly overhead.

He had fallen into a disturbed sleep when on waking up he found there was another occupant of the compartment. As thefts had been a common incident on the line specially in first class compartments, my friend switched on the electric light, the button of which was within his reach. This could be done without getting up.

In the glare of the electric light he saw distinctly his dying relation. He thought he was dreaming. He rubbed his eyes and then looked again. The apparition had vanished. He got up and looked out of the window. The train was passing through a station, without stopping. He could read the name of the station clearly. He opened his time table to find that he was still 148 miles from Calcutta.

Then he went to sleep again. In the morning he thought he had been dreaming. But he observed that the railway time table was still open at the place where he must have looked to ascertain the distance.

On reaching Calcutta he was told that his relation had died a few hours before his arrival.

My friend never related this to anybody till he knew that I was writing on the subject. This story, however, after what the professor saw loses its interest; and some suggested that it had better not be written at all. I only write this because this friend—who is also a relation of mine—is a well known Judicial Officer and would not have told this story unless it had been strictly true.

To the point is the following story which was in the papers about March 1914.

'In 1821 the Argyle Rooms* were patronised by the best people, the establishment being then noted for high-class musical entertainments. One evening in March, 1821, a young Miss M. with a party of friends, was at a concert in Argyle Rooms. Suddenly she uttered a cry and hid her face in her hands. She appeared to be suffering so acutely that her friends at once left the building with her and took her home. It was at first difficult to get the young lady to explain the cause of her sudden attack, but at last she confessed that she had been terrified by a horrible sight. While the concert was in progress she had happened to look down at the floor, and there lying at her feet she saw the corpse of a man. The body was covered with a cloth mantle, but the face was exposed, and she distinctly recognised the features of a friend, Sir J.Y.† On the following morning the family of the young lady received a message informing them that Sir J.Y. had been drowned the previous day in Southampton Water‡ through the capsizing of a boat, and that when his body was recovered it was entangled in a *boat cloak*. The

---

* Also seen as: "Argyll Rooms"; venue for concerts, masquerades, and other entertainments, open between 1806–1830.

† Corrected from Sir J.T. to "Sir J.Y." per original text: *A Portion of the Journal Kept by Thomas Raikes, Esq., from 1831 to 1847: Comprising Reminiscences of Social and Political Life in London and Paris During that Period.*

‡ Southampton River.

story of the Argyle Rooms apparition is told by Mr. Thomas Raikes[*] in his well-known diary, and he personally vouches for the truth of it.'[†]

In this connection the following cutting from an English paper of March, 1914, will be found very interesting and instructive.

'TALKS' WITH MR. STEAD.
SIR A. TURNER'S PSYCHIC EXPERIENCES.

General Sir Alfred Turner's psychic experiences, which he related to the London Spiritualist Alliance on May 7, in the salon of the Royal Society of British Artists, cover a very wide field, and they date from his early boyhood.

The most interesting and suggestive relate to the re-appearance of Mr. Stead[‡], says the *Daily Chronicle*. On the Sunday following the sinking of the Titanic, Sir Alfred was visiting a medium when she told him that on the glass of the picture behind his back the head of a man and afterwards 'its' whole form appeared. She described him minutely, and said he was holding a child by the hand. He had no doubt that it was Mr. Stead, and he wrote immediately to Miss Harper, Mr. Stead's private secretary. She replied saying that on the same day she had seen a similar apparition, in which Mr. Stead was holding a child by the hand.

A few days afterwards (continued Sir Alfred) at a private seance the voice of Stead came almost immediately and spoke at length. He told them what had happened in the last minutes of the wreck. All those who were on board when the vessel sank soon passed over,

---

[*] Thomas Raikes (1777–1848): British merchant banker, dandy, and diarist.

[†] The original date for this account by Raites was "about fifteen months prior to Dec. 26, 1832 (*not 1821*). The date of the drowning was actually May 5, 1831, as reported in the *Hampshire Telegraph*. Miss M is a "Miss Manningham;" the building was the "Hanover Square Rooms;" and that "the bodies of Sir J.Y., and two friends who were drowned with him were completely enveloped in their cloaks and greatcoats." These additional notes as recorded in: *Phantasms of the Living— Volume II*, by Edmund Gurney, Frederic Myers, Frank Podmore (1886).

[‡] William Thomas Stead (1849–1912): journalist, author, social reformer, and medium, who died on board the RMS *Titanic* (April 15, 1912).

but they had not the slightest notion that they were dead. Stead knew however, and he set to work to try and tell these poor people that they had passed over and that there was at any rate no more physical suffering for them. Shortly afterwards he was joined by other spirits, who took part in the missionary work.

Mr. Stead was asked to show himself to the circle. He said 'Not now, but at Cambridge House.' At the meeting which took place there, not everybody was sympathetic, and the results were poor, except that Mr. Stead came to them in short sharp flashes dressed exactly as he was when on earth.

Since then, said Sir Alfred, he had seen and conversed with Mr. Stead many times. When he had shown himself he had said very little, when he did not appear he said a great deal. On the occasion of his last appearance he said: 'I cannot speak to you. But pursue the truth. It is all truth.'

I am confident, Sir Alfred declared, that Mr. Stead will be of the greatest help to those of us who, on earth, work with him and to others who believe.

Extract from interior illustration of a séance in *The Fashionable Science of Parlour Magic* by John Henry Anderson (1855).

Uncredited engraving of lowering a bucket into a well.

THE BOY POSSESSED.

I THINK it was in 1906 that in one of the principle cities in India the son of a rich man became ill. He had high fever and delirium, and in his insensible state he was constantly talking in a language which was some kind of English but which the relatives could not understand. This boy was reading in one of the lower classes of a school and hardly knew the English language.

When the fever would not abate for twenty-four hours a doctor was sent for. The doctor arrived and went in to see the patient in the sick-room. The boy was lying on the bed with his eyes closed. It was nearly evening.

As soon as the doctor entered the sick-room the boy shouted, "Doctor—I am very hungry, order some food for me."

Of course, the doctor thought that the boy was in his senses. He did not know that the boy had not sufficient knowledge of the English language to express his ideas in that tongue. So the doctor asked his relations when he had taken food last. He was informed that the patient had had nothing to eat for the last eight or ten hours.

"What will you like to have?" asked the doctor.

"Roast mutton and plenty of vegetables," said the boy.

By this time the doctor had approached the bed-side, but it was too dark to see whether the eyes of the patient were open or not.

"But you are ill—roast mutton will do you harm," said the doctor.

"No it won't—I know what is good for me," replied the patient. At this stage the doctor was informed that the patient did not really know much English and that he was probably delirious. A suggestion was also made that probably he was possessed by a ghost.

The doctor who had been educated at the Calcutta Medical College[*] did not quite believe the ghost theory. He, however, asked the patient who he was.

In India, I do not know whether this is so in European countries too, lots of people are possessed by ghosts and the ghost speaks through his victim. So generally a question like this is asked by the exorcist, "Who are you and why are you troubling the poor patient?" The answer, I am told, is

---

[*] Now: Medical College and Hospital, Kolkata.

at once given and the ghost says what he wants. Of course I personally have never heard a ghost talk. I know a case in which a report was made to me that the wife of a groom of mine had become possessed by a ghost. On being asked what ghost it was, the woman was reported to have said, "the big ghost of the house across the drain." I ran to the out-houses to find out how much of it was true, but when I reached the stables the woman, I was told, was not talking. I found her in convulsions.

To return to our story; the doctor asked the patient who he was.

"I am General——," said the boy.

"Why are you here," asked the doctor.

"I shall tell you that after I have had my roast mutton and the vegetables—," replied the boy or rather the ghost.

"But how can we be convinced that you are really General——," asked the doctor.

"Call Captain X——of the XI Brahmans* and he will know, but in the meantime get me the food or I kill the patient."

The father of the patient at once began to shout that he would get the mutton and the vegetables at once. Meanwhile the Doctor had rushed out to procure some more medical assistance as well as to fetch Captain X of the XI Brahmans.

The few big European officers of the station were also informed, and within a couple of hours the sick-room was full of sensible educated gentlemen. The mutton too was by this time ready.

"The mutton is ready," said the doctor.

"Lower it into the well in the compound," said the boy.

A basket was procured and the mutton and the vegetables were lowered into the well. But scarcely had the basket gone down five yards (the well was forty feet deep) when somebody from inside the well shouted, "Take it away—take it away—there is no salt in it."

Those that were responsible for the preparation had to admit their mistake.

The basket was pulled out, some salt was put in, and the basket was lowered down again. But as the basket went in about five or six yards somebody from inside the well pulled it down with such force that the man who was lowering it narrowly escaped being dragged in; fortunately he let the rope slip through his hands with the result that though he did not fall

---

* Infantry regiment of the British Indian Army, often organized by caste (Brahmans), i.e. Bengals, Gurkhas, Punjabs, Sikhs, etc.

into the well his hands were bleeding profusely. Nothing happened after this near the well and everybody returned to the sick chamber.

After a few minutes' silence the patient said:—

"Take away the rope and the basket, why did you not tie the end of the rope to the post?"

"Why did you pull it so hard?" said one of the persons present.

"I was hungry and in a hurry," replied the patient.

They asked several persons to go down into the well but nobody would. At last a fishing hook was lowered down. The basket, which had at first completely disappeared, was now floating on the surface of the water. It was brought up, quite empty.

Captain X had in the meantime arrived and was taken to the patient. Two high officials of Government (both Europeans) had also arrived. As soon as the Captain stepped into the sick room the patient (we shall now call him the Ghost) said, "Good evening Captain X, these people will not believe that I am General—and I want to convince them."

The Captain was as much surprised as the others had been before.

"You may ask me anything you like Captain X, and I shall try to satisfy you," said the Ghost.

The Captain stood staring.

"Speak, Captain X,—are you dumb?" remarked the Ghost.

"I don't understand anything," stammered the Captain.

He was told everything by those present; and after hearing it the Captain formulated a question from one of the Military books. A correct reply was immediately given. Then followed a number of questions by the Captain, the replies to all of which were promptly given by the Ghost.

After this the Ghost said, "If you are all convinced, you may go now, and see me again tomorrow morning."

Everybody quietly withdrew.

The next morning there was a large gathering in the sick room. A number of European officers who had heard the story at the club on the previous evening dropped in. "Introduce each of these newcomers to me," said the Ghost.

Captain X introduced each person in due form.

"If anybody is curious to know anything I shall be glad to enlighten him," added the Ghost.

A few questions about England—position of buildings,—shops,— streets in London, were asked and correctly answered.

After all this catechizing[*], the Indian Doctor who had been in attendance asked, "Now, General, that we are fully convinced of your identity, why are you troubling this poor boy?"

"His father is rich," said the Ghost.

"Not very," replied the doctor, "but what do you want him to do?"

"My tomb at——pur has been destroyed by a branch of a tree falling upon it. I want that to be properly repaired," said the Ghost.

"I will get that done immediately," promised the father of the patient most eagerly.

"If you do that within a week I shall trouble your boy no longer," said the Ghost.

The monument was repaired accordingly and the boy has been never ill since.

This is the whole story; a portion of it appeared in the papers at the time; and there were several respectable witnesses whose testimony could not be impeached, though the whole thing is too wonderful.

Inexplicable as it is—it appears that dead persons are a bit jealous of the sanctity of their tombs. I have heard a story of a boy troubled by a Ghost who had inscribed his name on the tomb of a Mahommedan fakir[†]. His father had to repair the tomb and had to put an ornamental iron railing round it.

Somehow or other the thing looks like a fairy tale. The readers may have heard stories like this themselves and thought them as mere idle gossip.

I, therefore, reproduce here the whole of a letter as it appeared in "*The Leader*" of Allahabad, India—on the 15th July, 1913. The letter is written by a man, who, I think, understands quite well what he is saying.

A SUPERNATURAL PHENOMENON

Sir, It may probably interest your readers to read the account of a supernatural phenomenon that occurred, a few days ago, in the house of B. Rasiklal Mitra, B.A., district surveyor, Hamirpur. He has been living with his family in a bungalow for about a year. It is a good small bungalow, with two central and several side rooms. There is a verandah on the south and an enclosure, which serves the purpose of a court-yard for the ladies, on the north. On the eastern

---

[*] Archaic term for explaining something through questions and answers.

[†] Muslim fakir.

side of this enclosure is the kitchen and on the western, the privy. It has a big compound all round, on the south-west corner of which there is a tomb of some *Shahid*, known as the tomb of Phulan Shahid.

At about five o'clock in the evening on 26th June, 1913, when Mr. Mitra was out in office, it was suddenly noticed that the southern portion of the privy was on fire. People ran for rescue and by their timely assistance it was possible to completely extinguish the fire by means of water which they managed to get at the moment, before the fire could do any real damage. On learning of the fire, the ladies and children, all bewildered, collected in a room, ready to quit the building in case the fire was not checked or took a serious turn. About a square foot of the thatch was burnt. Shortly after this another corner of the house was seen burning. This was in the kitchen. It was not a continuation of the former fire as the latter had been completely extinguished. Not even smoke or a spark was left to kindle. The two places are completely separated from each other being divided by an open court-yard of thirty yards in length and there is no connection between them at all.

There was no fire at the time in the kitchen even, and there were no outsiders besides the ladies and children who were shut up in a room. This too was extinguished without any damage having been done. By this time Mr. Mitra and his several friends turned up on getting the news of the fire in his house. I was one of them. In short the fire broke out in the house at seven different places within an hour or an hour and a half; all these places situated so apart from one another that one was astonished to find how it broke out one after the other without any visible sign of the possibility of a fire from outside. We were all at a loss to account for the breaking out of the fire. To all appearance it broke out each time spontaneously and mysteriously. The fact that fire broke out so often as seven times within the short space of about an hour and a half, each time at a different place without doing any perceptible damage to the thatching of the bungalow or to any other article of the occupant of the house, is a mystery which remains to be solved. After the last breaking out, it was decided that the house must be vacated at once. Mr. Mitra and his family consequently removed to another house

---

* A martyr (in Islam).

of Padri[*] Ahmad Shah about two hundred yards distant therefrom. To the great astonishment of all nothing happened after the 'vacation' of the house for the whole night. Next morning Mr. Mitra came with his sister to have his morning meals prepared there, thinking that there was no fire during the night. To his great curiosity he found that the house was ablaze within ten or fifteen minutes of his arrival. They removed at once and everything was again all right. A day or two after he removed to a pucca[†] house within the town, not easy to catch fire. After settling his family in the new house Mr. Mitra went to a town (Moudha) some twenty-one miles from the headquarters. During the night following his departure, a daughter of Mr. Mitra aged about ten years saw in dream a boy who called himself Shahid Baba. The girl enquired of him about the reason of the fire breaking in her last residence and was told by him that she would witness curious scenes next morning, after which she would be told the remedy. Morning came and it was not long before fire broke out in the second storey of the new house. This was extinguished as easily as the previous ones and it did not cause any damage. Next came the turn of a dhoti of the girl mentioned above which was hanging in the house. Half of it was completely burnt down before the fire could be extinguished. In succession, the pillow wrapped in a bedding, a sheet of another bedding and lastly the dhoti which the girl was wearing caught fire and were extinguished after they were nearly half destroyed. Mr. Mitra's son aged about four months was lying on a cot: as soon as he was lifted up—a portion of the bed on which he was lying was seen burning. Although the pillow was burnt down there was no mark of fire on the bedding. Neither the girl nor the boy received any injury. Most curious of all, the papers enclosed in a box were burnt although the box remained closed. B. Ganesh Prasad, munsif[‡], and the post master hearing of this, went to the house and in their presence a mirzai[§] of the girl which was spread over a cot in the court-yard caught fire spontaneously and was seen burning.

---

[*] Type of priest or religious leader.

[†] Solid dwelling made of stone, brick, or other hardened material.

[‡] Magistrate.

[§] Garment similar to a jacket.

Now the girl went to sleep again. It was now about noon. She again saw the same boy in the dream. She was told this time that if the tomb was whitewashed and a promise to repair it within three months made, the trouble would cease. They were also ordained to return to the house which they had left. This command was soon obeyed by the troubled family which removed immediately after the tomb was whitewashed to the bungalow in which they are now peacefully living without the least disturbance or annoyance of any sort. I leave to your readers to draw their own conclusions according to their own experience of life and to form such opinion as they like.

PERMESHWAR DAYAL AMIST, B.A.,

Vakil, High Court
July 9.

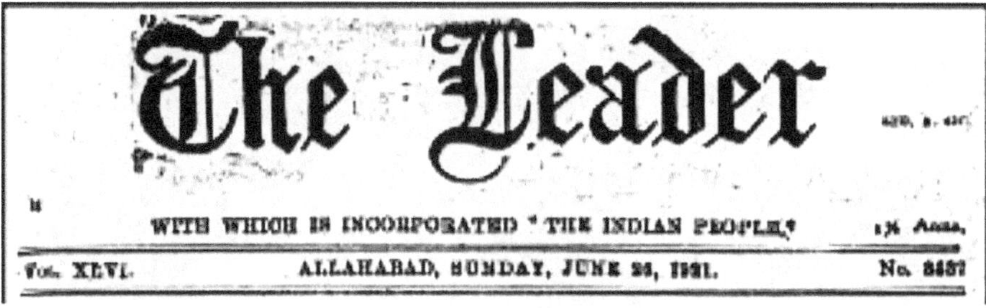

Heading of *The Leader* newspaper (published Allahabad, India), June 23, 1921 edition.

Uncredited Pahari painting of the 19th century
titled "Radha and Krishna Having Conversation."

THE EXAMINATION PAPER.

THIS is a story which I believe. Of course, this is not my personal experience; but it has been repeated by so many gentlemen, who should have witnessed the incident, with such wonderful accuracy that I cannot but believe it.

The thing happened at the Calcutta Medical College.

There was a student who had come from Dacca*, the Provincial Capital of Eastern Bengal. Let us call him Jogesh.

Jogesh was a handsome young fellow of about twenty-four. He was a married man and his wife's photograph stood in a frame on his table in the hostel. She was a girl hardly fifteen years old[†] and Jogesh was evidently very fond of her. Jogesh used to say a lot of things about his wife's attainments which we (I mean the other students of his class) believed, and a lot more which we did not believe. For instance we believed that she could cook a very good dinner, but that is an ordinary accomplishment of the average Bengali girl of her age.

Jogesh also said that she knew some mystic arts by means of which she could hold communion with him every night. Every morning when he came out of his room he used to say that his wife had been to him during the night and told him—this—that—and the other. This, of course, we did not believe, but as Jogesh was so sensitive we never betrayed our scepticism in his presence. But one significant fact happened one day which rather roused our curiosity.

One morning Jogesh came out with a sad expression and told us that his father was ill at home. His wife had informed him at night, he said; at that time we treated the matter with indifference but at about ten o'clock came a telegram (which we of course intercepted), intimating that his father was really ill.

The next morning Jogesh charged us with having intercepted his telegram; but we thought that he must have heard about the telegram from one of the students out of about half a dozen present when the telegram had arrived.

Jogesh's father, however, came round and the matter was forgotten.

Then came the annual University examination. Jogesh's weak subject

---

* Now Dhaka (capital of Bangladesh).

† Suggestive of arranged marriage; historically, most Indian females were married young (often pre-teen) in ceremony and alliance only; consummation was not permitted until both husband and wife were "of age," and the wife remained living with her parents in the meantime.

was *Materia Medica*[*] and everybody knew it. So we suggested that Jogesh should ask his wife what questions would be set, during one of her nightly visits.

After great hesitation Jogesh consented to ask his wife on the night before the examination.

The eventful night came and went. In the morning Jogesh appeared crestfallen and we anxiously inquired what his wife had said.

"She told me the questions," answered Jogesh with a rueful countenance, "but she added she would never visit me again here."

The questions were of greater importance and so we wanted to have a look at them. Jogesh had noted these down on the back of a theatre programme (or hand bill—I really forget which) and showed the questions to us. There were eleven of them—all likely questions such as Major—— might ask. To take the questions down and to learn the answers was the work of an hour, and in spite of our scepticism we did it. And we were glad that we did it.

When the paper was distributed, we found that the questions were identically those which we had seen that very morning and the answers to which we had prepared with so much labour only a few hours before.

The matter came to the notice of the authorities who were all European gentlemen. The eleven answer papers were examined and re-examined, and finally Jogesh was sent for by Col.——the Principal to state how much truth was there in what had been reported, but Jogesh prudently refused to answer the question; and finally the Colonel said that it was all nonsense and that the eleven students knew their Materia Medica very well and that was all. In fact it was the Colonel himself who had taught the subject to his students, and he assured all the eleven students that he was really proud of them. The ten students were however proud of Jogesh and his mystic wife. It was decided that a subscription should be raised and a gold necklace should be presented to Jogesh's wife as a humble token of respect and gratitude of some thankful friends, and this plan was duly executed.

Jogesh is now a full-fledged doctor and so are all the other ten who had got hold of the Materia Medica paper in that miraculous way.

After the incident of that night Jogesh's wife had an attack of brain fever and for some time her life was despaired of, and we were all so sorry. But,

---

[*] Latin for "Medical Material," meaning the sources and properties of therapeutic or pharmaceutic healing (ingredients of drugs/medicine).

thank God, she came round after a long and protracted illness, and then we sent her the necklace.

Jogesh subsequently with great reluctance thus divulged the secret to us. His wife had given him an Indian charm-case with instructions to put it on with a chain round the neck whenever he required her. Immediately he put on the chain, to which this charm-case was attached, round his neck, he felt as if he was in a trance and then his wife came. Whether she came in the flesh or only in spirit Jogesh could not say as he never had the opportunity of touching her so long as she was there, for he could not get up from the bed or the chair or wherever he happened to be. On the last occasion she had entreated him not to press her to tell the questions. He had, however, insisted and so she had dictated to him the examination paper as if from memory. The theatre programme was the only thing within his reach and he had taken down all the questions on that, as he thought he could not rely upon his own memory. Then she had walked up to him, unbuttoned his *kurta* (native shirt)[*] at the chin, and removed the charm-case from the chain to which it was attached. When she had vanished, the charm-case had vanished too. The chain had, of course, remained on Jogesh's neck. Since that eventful night Jogesh had had no mystic communion with his wife during his stay in Calcutta.

She refused to discuss the subject when Jogesh afterwards met her at Dacca. So the mystery remains unsolved.

Talking of questions and answers reminds me of an incident that took place on one occasion in my presence.

A certain Mohammedan hypnotist once visited us when I was at College.

There was a number of us, all students, in the hostel common-room or library when this man came and introduced himself to us as a professional hypnotist. On being asked whether he could show us anything wonderful and convincing he said he could. He asked us to procure a teapoy with three strong legs. This we did. Then he asked two of us to sit round that small table and he also sat down himself. He asked us to put our hands flat on the table and think of some dead person. We thought of a dead friend of ours. After we had thus been seated for about five minutes there was a rap on the leg of the teapoy. We thought that the hypnotist had kicked the leg on his side.

"The spirit has come," said the hypnotist.

---

[*] Loose collarless shirt or tunic (usually cotton or silk).

"How should we ascertain?" I asked.

"Ask him some question and he will answer," said the hypnotist.

Then we asked how many from our class would obtain the University degree that year.

"Spirit," said the hypnotist, "as the names are mentioned one rap means pass, two mean plucked*"; then he addressed the others sitting around. "See that I am not kicking at the leg of the teapoy."

Half a dozen of the boys sat down on the floor to watch.

As each name was mentioned there came one rap or two raps as the case might be till the whole list was exhausted.

"We can't ascertain the truth of this until three months are over," said I.

"How many rupees have I in my pocket?" asked one of the lookers-on.

There came three distinct raps and on examining the purse of the person we found that he had exactly three rupees and nothing more.

Then we asked a few more questions, and the answers came promptly in "*Yes*" or "*No*" by means of raps.

Then according to the hypnotist's suggestion one student wrote a line from Shakespeare and the ghost was asked what those lines were.

"As the plays are named rap once at the name of the play from which the passage has been taken," said the hypnotist, solemnly addressing the Spirit.

"Hamlet."

No reply.

"King Lear."

No reply.

"Merchant of Venice."

No reply.

"Macbeth."

One loud rap.

"Macbeth," said the hypnotist. "Now which Act?"

"Act I."

No reply.

"Act II."

No reply.

"Act III."

No reply.

"Act IV."

---

* Failing (in examinations).

No reply.
"Act V."
One loud rap.
"Scene I."
No reply.
"Scene II."
No reply.
"Scene III."
One loud rap.
"Now what about the lines," said the hypnotist.
"Line One—Two—Three . . . Thirty-nine."
No reply.
"Forty."
One loud rap.
"Forty-one."
One loud rap.
"Forty-two."
One loud rap.
"Forty-three."
One loud rap.
"Forty-four."
One loud rap.
"Forty-five."
One loud rap.
"Forty-six."
No reply.
A copy of Shakespeare's *Macbeth* was at once procured and opened at Act V, Sec. III, line 40.

> "Can'st thou not minister to a mind diseas'd,
> Pluck from the memory a rooted sorrow,
> Raze out the written troubles of the brain,
> And with some sweet oblivious antidote,
> Cleanse the stuff'd bosom of that perilous stuff,
> Which weighs upon the heart?"

This was what we read.
The student was then asked to produce his paper and on it was the identical quotation.

Then the hypnotist asked us to remove our hands from the top of the teapoy. The hypnotist did the same thing and said, "The Spirit has gone."

We all stared at each other in mute surprise.

Afterwards we organized a big show for the benefit of the hypnotist, and that was a grand success.

Lots of strange phenomena were shown to us which are too numerous to mention. The fellows who had sat on the floor watching whether or not it was the hypnotist who was kicking at the leg of the teapoy assured us that he was not.

The strange feats of this man (hypnotist, clairvoyant, and thought-reader all rolled into one) have ever since remained an insoluble mystery.

Uncredited illustration, "Brahmin students" from the *Illustrated London News*, 1858.

Woodblock print of Kali, the Hindu goddess of
death, by Nritya Lal Datta (ca. 1860–1870).

THE MESSENGER OF DEATH.

WE have often been told how some of us receive in an unlooked-for manner an intimation of death some time before that incident does actually occur.

The late Mr. W.T. Stead[*], for instance, before he sailed for America in the Titanic had made his will and given his friends clearly to understand that he would see England no more.

Others have also had such occult premonitions, so to say, a few days, and sometimes weeks before their death.

We also know a number of cases in which people have received similar intimation of the approaching death of a near relation or a dear friend who, in most cases, lives at a distance.

There is a well-known family in England (one of the peers of the realm) in whose case previous intimation of death comes in a peculiar form. Generally when the family is at dinner a carriage is heard to drive up to the portico. Everybody thinks it is some absent guest who has arrived late and my lord or my lady gets up to see who it is. Then when the hall door is opened it is seen that there is no carriage at all. This is a sure indication of an impending death in the family.

I know another very peculiar instance. A certain gentleman in Bengal died leaving four sons and a widow. The youngest was about five years old. These children used to live with their mother in the family residence under the guardianship of their uncle.

One night the widow had a peculiar dream. It seemed to her that her husband had returned from a long journey for an hour or so and was going away again. Of course, in her dream the lady forgot all about her widowhood.

Before his departure the husband proposed that she should allow him to take one of the sons with him and she might keep the rest.

The widow readily agreed and it was settled that the youngest but one[†] should go with the husband. The boy was called, and he very willingly agreed to go with his father. The mother gave him a last hug and kiss and passed him on to the father who carried him away.

---

[*] William Thomas Stead, English newspaper editor and investigative journalist.
[†] Second youngest.

The next moment the widow woke. She remembered every particular of the dream. A cold sweat stood on her forehead when she comprehended what she had done.

The boy died the next morning. As she told me the story she added that the only consolation she had was that the child was safe with his father. A very poor consolation indeed!

Now this is a peculiar story told in a peculiar fashion; but I know one or two wonderful stories which are more peculiar still.

It is a custom in certain families in Bengal that in connection with the annual *Durga pooja*, black male goats are offered as a sacrifice. In certain other families strictly vegetarian offerings are made.

The mode of sacrificing the goat is well known to some readers, and will not interest those who do not know the custom. The fact remains that millions of goats are sacrificed all over Bengal during the three days of the *Durga pooja* and on the *Shyama pooja** night (i.e. *Diwali* or *Dipavali*).

There is however nothing ominous in all this, except when the "sacrificial sword" fails to sever the head of the goat from the trunk at one deadly stroke. As this bodes ill the householder to appease the deity, to whose wrath such failure is attributed, sacrifices another goat then and there and further offers to do penance by sacrificing double the number of goats next year.

But what is more pertinent to the subject I am dealing with is the sacrificing of goats under peculiar circumstances. Thus when an epidemic (such as cholera, small pox and now probably plague) breaks out in a village in Bengal all the principal residents of the place in order to propitiate the deity to whose curse or ire the visitation is supposed to be due, raise a sufficient amount by subscription for worshipping the irate Goddess. The black he-goat that is offered as a sacrifice on such an occasion is not actually slain, but being besmeared with "*Sindur*" (red oxide of mercury) and generally having one of the ears cropped or bored is let loose, *i.e.* allowed to roam about until clandestinely passed on to some neighbouring village, to which the goat is credited with the virtue of transferring the epidemic from the village originally infected. The goats thus marked are not looked upon

---

* Festival and celebration of Kali, a major Hindu goddess (Mother Goddess), most frequently associated with death, but also with time, change, creation, and destruction; similar to *Durga pooja*, festival and celebration of Durga, the Hindu goddess of strength, motherhood, and wars.

with particular favour in the villages. They are generally not ill-treated by the villagers, and when they eat up the cabbages, etc., all that the poor villagers can do is to curse them and drive them away—but they return as soon as the poor owner of the garden has moved away. Such goats become, in consequence, very bold and give a lot of trouble.

When, therefore, such a billy-goat appears in a village, what the villagers generally do is to hire a boat, carry the goat a long distance along the river, say twenty or twenty-five miles and leave him there. Now the villagers of the place where such a goat is left play the same trick, so it sometimes happens that the goat comes back after a week or so.

Once it so happened that a dedicated goat made his unwelcome appearance in a certain village in Bengal. The villagers hired a boat and carried him about twenty miles up the river and left him there. The goat came back after a week. Then they left him at a place twenty miles down the river and he came back again. Afterwards they took the goat fifty miles up and down the river but each time the goat returned like the proverbial bad penny.

After trying all kinds of tricks in their attempt to get rid of the goat the villagers became desperate. So a few hot-headed young men of the village in an evil hour decided to kill the goat. Instead of killing the goat quietly (as probably they should have done) and throwing the carcass into the river, they organised a grand feast and ate the flesh of the dedicated goat.

Within twenty-four hours of the dinner each one of them who had taken part in it was attacked with cholera of a most virulent type and within another twenty-four hours every one of them was dead. Medical and scientific experts were called in from Calcutta to explain the cause of the calamity, but no definite results were obtained from these investigations. One thing, however, was certain. There was no poison of any kind in the food.

The cause of the death of about thirty young men remains a mystery. This was retribution with a vengeance and the writer does not see the justice of the divine providence in this particular case.

In another village the visit of the messenger of death was also marked in a peculiar fashion.

Two men one tall and the other short, the tall man carrying a lantern, are seen to enter the house of one of the villagers late in the evening; and the next morning there is a death in the house which they entered overnight.

When, for the first time, these two mysterious individuals were seen to enter a house, an alarm of thieves was raised. The house was searched but no trace of any stranger was found in the house. The poor villager who had given the alarm was publicly scolded for his folly after the fruitless search, for thinking that thieves would come with a lighted lantern. But that poor man had mentioned the lighted lantern before the search commenced and nobody had thought that fact "*absurd*" at that time.

Since that date a number of people have seen these messengers of death enter the houses of several persons, and whenever they enter a house, a death takes place in that house within the next twenty-four hours.

Some of the witnesses who have seen these messengers of death are too cautious and too respectable to be disbelieved or doubted. Your humble servant on one occasion passed a long time in this village, but he, fortunately or unfortunately, call it what you please, never saw these fell messengers of death.

In another family in Bengal death of a member is foretold a couple of days before the event in a very peculiar manner.

This is a very rich family having a large residential house with a private temple or chapel attached to it, but the members never pay a penny to the doctor or the chemist either.

In many rich families in Bengal there are private deities the worship of which is conducted by the heads of the families assisted by the family priests. There are generally private temples adjoining the houses or rooms set apart for such idols, and all the members of the family and especially the ladies say their prayers there.

Such a temple remains open during the day and is kept securely closed at night, because nobody should be allowed to disturb the deity at night and also because there is generally a lot of gold and silver articles in the temple which an unorthodox thief may carry away.

Now what I have just mentioned was the custom of the particular household referred to above.

One night a peculiar groan was heard issuing from the temple. All the inmates of the house came out to see what the matter was. The key of the temple was with the family priest who was not present. He had probably gone to some other person's house to have a smoke and a chat, and it was an hour before the key could be procured and the door of the temple opened.

Everything was just as it had been left three or four hours previously. The cause or origin of the groans was never traced or discovered.

The next morning one of the members of the family was suddenly taken ill and died before medical aid could be obtained from Calcutta.

This was about fifty years ago. Since then the members of this family have become rather accustomed to these groans.

If there is a case of real Asiatic cholera or a case of double pneumonia they don't call in a doctor though there is a very capable and learned medical man within a mile. But if once the groans are heard the person, who gets the smallest pin-prick the next morning, dies; and no medical science has ever done any good.

"The most terrible thing in this connection is the suspense," said one of the members of that family to me once. "As a rule you hear the groans at night and then you have to wait till the morning to ascertain whose turn it is. Generally however you find long before sunrise that somebody has become very ill. If not, you have to wire to all the absent members of the family in the morning to enquire—what you can guess. And you have to await the replies to the telegrams. How the minutes pass between the hearing of the groans till it is actually ascertained who is going to die—need not be described."

"You must have been having an exciting time of it," I asked this young man.

"Generally not, because we find that somebody is ill from before and then we know what is going to happen," replied my informant.

"But during your experience of twenty-five years you must have been very nervous about these groans yourself at times," I asked.

"On two occasions only we had to be nervous because nobody was ill beforehand; but in each case that person died who was the most afraid. I was not nervous on these occasions myself for some reason or other."

These uncanny groans of the messenger of death have remained a mystery, though their tone has been "caught with Death's prophetic ear" by the victims and their friends for the last fifty years.

I know another family in which the death of the head of the family is predicted in a very peculiar manner.

There is a big picture of the Goddess Kali in the family. On the night of the *Shyama pooja* (*Dewali*) which occurs about the middle of November, this picture is brought out and worshipped.

The picture is a big oil painting of the old Indian School and has a massive solid gold frame. The picture is a thing of beauty—worth seeing—

and is a joy for ever to the family.

All the year round it hangs on the eastern wall of the room occupied by the head of the family.

Now the peculiar thing with this family is that no male member of the family dies out of his turn. The eldest male member dies leaving behind everybody else. The next man then becomes the eldest and dies afterwards and so on.

But before the death of the head of the family the warning comes in a peculiar way.

The picture of the goddess is found hanging upside down. One morning when the head of the family comes out of his bedroom and the youngsters go in to make the room tidy, as they call it (though they generally make the room more untidy and finally leave it to the servants), they find the famous family picture hanging literally topsy-turvy (that is, with head downwards) and they at once sound the alarm. Then every one knows that the head of the family is doomed and will die within a week.

This fact, however, does not disturb the normal quiet of the family. Because the *pater familias** is generally very old and infirm and more generally quite prepared to die.

But the fact remains that so long as the warning does not come in this peculiar fashion every member of the household knows that there is no immediate danger.

For instance, it is only when this warning comes that all the children who are out of the station, are wired for.

Every reader must admit that this is rather weird.

Apropos of the above incident I may cite the following observations of Mr. Reginald B. Span in "the *Occult Review* of April 1915" to which my attention has been drawn since the publication of the Second Edition:—

> The strong belief that formerly prevailed in the efficacy of sympathetic cures can scarcely have existed without some foundation, nor are they more extraordinary than the sympathetic falling of pictures and the stopping of clocks and watches connected with deaths and disasters in the families of the owners. There are numerous well-attested cases extant of such occurrences, and some well-known physiologists pronounce the

---

* Latin: father of the family.

phenomenon indisputable. A curious instance in point was the stopping of "Big Ben" at the very time its maker died. Pictures falling before or at the deaths of their owners, or some member of the household, have been noticed over and over again in all parts of the world.

Untitled watercolor in the Patna style by Sevak Ram depicting the sacrifice of a black goat during celebration of *Durga puja* (*Durga pooja*).

Uncredited gilded painting from the 19th century (state of Tamil Nadu), depicting Parashurama slaying the Haihaya King Kartavirya Arjuna.

POSTSCRIPT
IN LIEU OF PREFACE

IN bringing out a third edition I can not help observing that the recent downfall of the German Empire*, which—though richly deserved—might have been prevented if her proud and despotic ruler had not culpably neglected the warnings of the "White Lady" as detailed at the close of a former Preface, amply proves that the appearance of that mysterious Lady or that of any other Unearthly Visitor was intended not merely to adorn a tale, but sometimes to point a moral also.

There was a time when an educated gentleman was ashamed to admit that "the sheeted dead did squeak and gibber in the Roman streets."† But those days are gone by. And in the present stage of our spiritual knowledge no one could boldly assert that the phenomena described in these pages were utterly improbable.

S.M.

Feb. 9th, 1919.

THE END.

---

* World War I.

† Horatio: *Hamlet* by William Shakespeare (Act 1, Scene 1).

ADVERTISEMENTS
(PER SECOND EDITION, 1917)

BY THE SAME AUTHOR.

THE
MYSTERIOUS TRADERS

Being the adventures of a gang of swindlers who robbed the rich only.

PRICE SIX ANNAS.

Of all Booksellers, and of Railway Bookstalls.

ALLAHABAD:

A.H. WHEELER & CO.

SIXTH EDITION JUST OUT.

Mr. and Mrs. JOHN BROWN AT HOME

A series of amusing sketches of Station Life in India.

ONE RUPEE.

Of all Booksellers, and of Railway Bookstalls.

ALLAHABAD:

A.H. WHEELER & CO.

ADVERTISEMENTS
(PER FOURTH EDITION, 1921)

LIST OF BOOKS PUBLISHED BY A.H. WHEELER & CO.

TOLD IN THE VERANDAH.
Passage in the life of Colonel Bowlong, set
down by his Adjutant .　　　.　　　.　　　.　　　Rs. 2-8.˙

INDIAN GHOST STORIES.
By S. Mukerji, author of "The Mysterious Traders"　　　Rs. 1-8.

Mr. and Mrs. JOHN BROWN "AT HOME."
By John Brown. A series of eighteen sketches
of station life in India .　　　.　　　.　　　.　　　Re. 1.

THE YELLOW LINE.
By Victor Shea　　　.　　　.　　　.　　　.　　　Rs. 1-8.
A collection of short stories, some of which
have appeared in London periodicals and now
collected in one volume. Ask to see it when
next at any of Wheeler's Bookstalls.

WARLIKE SNIPS AND SNAPS.
Letters written by Babu Piche Lal, B.A.,
from Mesopotamia. Illustrated.　　　.　　　.　　　Rs. 2.

MORE SNIPS AND SNAPS.
By the author of "Warlike Snips and Snaps."
In the Press. Price about　　　.　　　.　　　.　　　Rs. 2·8.

EXCURSIONS IN INK.
By R. J. Minney, author of "The Night Life of
Calcutta." Illustrated. *In the Press.*

MEETING THE SUN.
By Louis Tracy. Written on his arrival in India.
Full of good stories about India　　　.　　　.　　　Rs. 2.

ROYAL AUCTION BRIDGE.
Robertson's Pocket Guide to the Laws and
Penalties of Royal Auction Bridge　　　.　　　Re. 1.

˙ Rs.: Rupees (or, Re: Rupee).

EAST & WEST.

VOL. XII.   DECEMBER, 1913.   No. 146.

A WINGED POET.

" I see a chariot like that thinnest boat,
  In which the mother of the months is borne
  By ebbing night into her western cave,

Within it sits a winged infant, white
  Its countenance, like the whiteness of bright snow,
  Its plumes are as feathers of sunny frost
  Its limbs gleam white, through the wind-flowing folds
  Of its white robe, woof of ethereal pearl.

                          . . . . . in its hand
  It sways a quivering moonbeam, from whose point
  A guiding power directs the chariot's prow
  Over its wheeléd clouds, which as they roll
  Over the grass, and flowers, and waves, wake sounds
  Sweet as a singing rain of silver dew."

SHELLEY, from *Prometheus Unbound.*

WHEN he wrote these lines Shelley limned unconsciously the genius of his own poetry—a winged child etherealised.

Readers of Francis Thompson's Essay on Shelley, a poet's tribute to a brother-poet, will remember that Mr. Thompson pronounced Shelley to be, as poet and man, essentially a child. " To be a child," he wrote, " is to believe in love, in loveliness, in *belief*; it is to live in a nutshell and to count yourself the king of infinite space." " To the last Shelley retained the

Journal cover of *East & West*, vol. XII, issue 146, (December, 1913):
magazine of first publication for *The Mysterious Traders*.

THE MYSTERIOUS TRADERS
(A Detective Thriller)[*]
Publication Notes

DESCRIBED by publisher A.H. Wheeler & Co. as "Being the adventures of a gang of swindlers who robbed the rich only," *The Mysterious Traders* was originally serialized in three parts and included in the following journal issues:

"The Mysterious Traders: I.—The Diamonds" by S.N. Mukerji. *East & West*, *XII*(144), 925–934, October, 1913.

"The Mysterious Traders: II.—The Pictures" by S.N. Mukerji. *East & West*, *XII*(145), 1015–1025, November, 1913.

"The Mysterious Traders: III.—The Doctor" by S.N. Mukerji. *East & West*, *XII*(146), 1129–1137, December, 1913.

The stories were then combined into one full book-length edition, titled *The Mysterious Traders*, and published by A.H. Wheeler & Co. (Allahabad, India) in 1915.

As far as this editor is aware, after the 1915 run, *The Mysterious Traders* fell out of print, and remained so, until being republished for the first time in over a century (utilizing the original serialized text) within this subject book *The Collected Works of S. Mukerji*!

---

[*] Parenthetical element is addition from this editor and not part of original title.

Uncredited lithograph in *The Sartorial Art Journal* reflecting various styles of men's fashion in August, 1899.

THE MYSTERIOUS TRADERS

(Messrs. Hornby, Hunter & Co.)

I.—THE DIAMONDS.

THIS company of mysterious traders was started by five gentlemen of high character and talents, who combined together with the intention of carrying on a lucrative business for the benefit of the public. The subscribed capital was £20 by each member, that is, £100 in all. But at the end of the first financial year of the company it was found that, besides a monthly allowance of £30 that each member received, there was a net profit of £150,000 free from income tax for distribution among the shareholders, who were of course only five in number.

But before proceeding, I think it is only fair that I should tell the reader something about the previous life of the shareholders, who were the directors as well as promoters of this company.

1. Dr. John Hornby.—This gentleman was a qualified medical man with a diploma and a certificate, and was once badly wanted by the Police of America in connection with a case of suspected poisoning. The Doctor thought that prudence was the better part of valour, and moreover he did not like the publicity and scandal of a trial, and so he quietly came away to England to practise in medicine there.

2. Mr. James Hunter.—This gentleman was the chief repairer in a firm of jewellers and watchmakers in America. He was at first only an ordinary watchmaker, and was employed by the firm on a small salary. He was afterwards made the chief man in the establishment and once upon a time he, by mistake of course, delivered a $2,000 repeater[*], which had been entrusted to him for oiling and cleaning, to the wrong person. It was also alleged that he had received $200 as repairing charges from the person to whom this watch was delivered (which amount he had put by an equally sad mistake in his own pocket instead of his employers' cash-box). All this was, however, never proved against him, and lawfully we must deem a man innocent till he is actually proved to be guilty. It was a very shady

---

[*] High-end watch that chimed the hours (and minutes, depending on type), allowing for the telling of time in the dark (i.e. this before artificial illumination).

transaction on the whole, and Mr. Hunter, like Dr. Hornby, did not care for a public scandal. He crossed the Atlantic and came over to England to earn his honest bread. But he had sworn that he would return to his employers every dollar of the money which he had borrowed from them, and further that he would make good the damages which the firm had to incur in satisfying the enraged customer, whose watch was not forthcoming.

3. Mr. Smith Carman.—This gentleman was a railway guard in America. Once by a pure mistake he took a bag left behind in a train by a lady to his own house instead of depositing it in the lost property office. As he was rather curious to see the contents, he opened the bag and found that besides other articles of practically no value there was a leather case, which must have contained a necklace. He returned everything as he had found it to the office, but the owner of the bag declared that the necklace box was not empty when the bag was left in the train. Instead of being grateful for the safe return of her bag, this lady told the police that she suspected theft. Mr. Carman at the same time found that he had important business on the other side of the Atlantic. The necklace, we are told, was never found.

4. Mr. Francis Little.—This gentleman was of very little importance in the States. Once while paying a tobacconist a dollar for a few cigars, he produced a $100 bank note and the tobacconist, foolish man, suspected that something was wrong. He handed over the note to a police officer who was, as fortune would have it, present at the shop. As the police officer was scrutinising the note, as every stupid police officer does scrutinise everything which is of no importance, Mr. Little found the atmosphere of the shop too stuffy and so he walked out of the shop, but in his hurry forgot to take the change or the box of cigars either. When the police officer and the tobacconist came out to look for Mr. Little with a view probably to return him the change, they found that Mr. Little was not visible. It subsequently transpired that only a few minutes before the incident recorded above, Mr. Little had purchased a $10 watch from a jeweller's shop in the same street and had paid in cash in a $100 note, receiving $90 in exchange. Another jeweller also swore that Mr. Little had purchased a $10 ring from him and received $90 in exchange for a $100 note. All these notes were subsequently taken possession of by the police, but what they did with them has not yet transpired.

5. Mr. Thomas Rider.—This gentleman was a keen bicyclist. Passing along the street one day he found a bicycle on the road side. The owner had

gone inside the shop to make purchases. The keen cyclist's instinct must have told Mr. Rider that the bicycle was worth $50 as it stood. He thought he would have a little spin and return in plenty of time, in fact, long before the owner came out after making his purchases. He rode away but before he had gone a couple of miles, he found that he was feeling very thirsty and so dismounted for a drink. But he also discovered to his annoyance that he had left his purse at home. As he found it simply impossible to go a step further without a drink, he pawned the bike for $40 and put the money in his pocket. He had, of course, every intention of returning for the machine and restoring it to its owner, but he was informed the next morning that the bike had been taken possession of by the police, and so he had no opportunity of redeeming it. A second transaction of the same nature was successfully carried through but then Mr. Rider found that the impertinent police officers resented any man's riding away on a bike which he had not paid for. And so Mr. Rider came away to England to practise cycling in the streets of London.

These were the gentlemen of the most immaculate character, who engineered the firm of Messrs. Hornby, Hunter & Co.

Having started the firm on a sound financial basis with its unregistered head office in a certain London flat, the promoters of the company decided to do a fast and lucrative business.

The first meeting of the shareholders took place on the first day of April 1902, and on that memorable day the directors decided what their first business transaction should be. It was proposed, seconded and unanimously agreed that their first transaction should be in diamonds, and diamonds of the first water*. But £100 were found too little to purchase the Countess of Newford's diamond necklace. Mr. Hunter had seen this necklace, and had assessed it at £45,000, but the lady would give them no credit. Moreover, they found that she was unwilling to sell her necklace for any price. It was, she said, an heirloom, and she would not part with it for any price. There were three pink stones in it, the like of which did not exist in England, and naturally the Countess of Newford was very fond of making a show of them.

There was a ball at the town house of the Countess of Sutherland, and of course the Countess of Newford was there, brilliant, shining, cheerful and happy. She was a lady of thirty-five and looked much younger. She was the daughter of a very respectable country gentleman of Sussex, and the Earl had

---

* Archaic term for "of the finest quality."

married her for her beauty fifteen years ago. He and been a very kind husband, and she had been a very loving and dutiful wife. She was very proud of her husband who denied her nothing, she was very proud of her two daughters who were very beautiful too, and were learning music and painting and French in Paris; she was also very proud of her two sons who lived in the ancestral Hall at Newford and who had smashed up into atoms nearly all the old china that lay within their reach and of which their great grandfather was very fond; she was very proud of her horses and her motor cars of which she had any number, and lastly she was immensely proud of the Newford diamonds which everybody said were worth £60,000, and which Messrs. Hornby, Hunter & Co. assessed at £45,000.

The Earl of Newford, who was a very important man in the Cabinet, was sent for by the Prime Minister at the last moment, and as he loved politics more than dancing, he asked his wife to go alone and tell the Countess of Sutherland that he would be there without fail but would be late.

"Where is your husband, Nora dear?" was the cheerful greeting of the Countess of Sutherland when she found that Lord Newford had not come.

"He will be here in an hour, Emma," said Lady Newford. "He was sent for by the Prime Minister at the last moment, and he said that he would be here in an hour."

"Oh, Lord Newford's hour means two hundred minutes," said Miss Spencer, the daughter of the Cotton King[*]. "I am sure he will turn up when we are all leaving."

"How beautiful you are looking tonight, Nora," observed Lady Sutherland. "Your necklace is simply glorious."

"It is a famous necklace, is it not?" said Miss Spencer. "Father says it is worth the ransom of a king."

"It has been in our family for the last one hundred years, and it is supposed to bring us good luck," said the Countess of Newford smiling.

Lady Sutherland went to look after her other guests, and Lady Newford was joined by Sir John Martin, the young Baronet[†], whose father was once a poor engineer but having hit upon a new silent engine for motor cars, had died at the age of sixty a Baronet and a millionaire.

---

[*] Not an uncommon moniker for someone successfully involved in speculation in the cotton markets.

[†] Hereditary title, one rank below Baron, that could be purchased by "gentlemen of good birth with (substantial) income" and allows for the address of "sir."

"How is your new car going," asked the Baronet, who was like his father a keen mechanical engineer himself.

"Exceedingly well, Sir John," said the Countess. "I like it better than all the other cars that I have got."

I fitted it up with the self-starting machinery with my own hands," said the Baronet, who took great pride in his own engineering skill. "Have you ever driven the car yourself, Lady Newford?"

"I tried once and nearly killed a man, and I have not tried driving since."

"Where was that," asked the Baronet, who had once had to pay thirty shillings himself for exceeding the speed limit.

"Why, here in London."

"I think if you want to practise driving yourself you should begin in the country; broad roads, no people to get crushed, no carriages to collide with, no cars of greater power to give you the benefit of the dust," suggested the Baronet.

"Yes, I shall take the car with me at the end of the season and try," said the Countess.

"You have not got a small car; begin with a small two-seater," said the Baronet.

"Talking of motor cars," interrupted Miss Spencer, who had come up unobserved, "I say, Sir John, now that you are an engineer, tell me what kind of motorist shall I make?"

"Well, you will be able to kill a man in the first attempt," smiled the Baronet, "that is, if you do not kill yourself first."

"You are a very wicked man—and your prognostication about Mr. O'Donnell came true," said Miss Spencer.

"O'Donnell was too rash and what I said anybody else could have said," laughed the Baronet.

Then they all parted, the dancing had commenced and both the Countess and the Baronet were keen dancers and so was Miss Spencer.

Everything passed off peacefully and uneventfully till eleven o'clock. The Earl of Newford had not yet arrived, but nobody was anxious as everybody who knew the Earl knew that when he went to the Prime Minister he was always late for every other engagement.

At 11.30 there was a slight stir among the Countess of Newford's group and a gentleman, fair, fat and forty, dressed in immaculate evening suit with an abundance of gold chain, from which dangled a masonic charm set with enormous diamonds, came and bowed to the Countess and said in a most confidential whisper that he would like to speak to her ladyship on an important private matter, which was very urgent and could not brook delay.

The Countess of Newford had never seen this gentleman before, but she felt from the tone that he had something very important indeed to communicate. She followed him to the hall and thence to the stairs, where this gentleman informed her that while coming from the Prime Minister's house to that of the Countess of Sutherland, the Earl's chauffeur had smashed up the car, got killed himself and nearly killed his master. That passing along the road in his own car the gentleman, being a medical man himself, had picked up the Earl, and had carried him to his residence where he was lying in a most precarious condition.

I came in my car to take you to him with all possible speed," said the stranger, and we shall go as fast as we can.

They got inside the car, which was a very commodious and silent Daimler Landaulette, and started.

"Is he much hurt?" asked the Countess.

"He is badly injured, but I have not examined him thoroughly yet," said the other. "I thought it my duty to inform you first. I have however telephoned for Dr. Crawford, and he will have arrived by now."

"I am afraid I do not exactly know er—er—"

"I am Dr. Richard Green of——"

"I beg your pardon, I have heard your name but this is the first time that we have met."

"I am afraid I never had the honour of meeting your ladyship before."

They were silent the rest of the way.

They reached Dr. Green's house. The Countess was too nervous to observe which way they had come or in what part of the town they were.

The doctor helped her out of the car, and they entered a well-furnished hall, and the well-dressed footman conducted them to the drawing-room where the Countess dropped into a chair. Dr. Green went to his surgery which was adjoining. There he met Dr. Crawford, who had arrived in the meantime and examined the patient.

"His condition is critical, Green," said Dr. Crawford in a low tone. "I am afraid he will not last long."

"Speak low," said Dr. Green, "his wife is here, and I am sure she has not got very strong nerves."

"We must break the news very gently to her," said Dr. Crawford. The Countess was, however, overhearing the conversation as the door between the two rooms had been accidentally left open by Dr. Green when he had passed out of the drawing-room. When Dr. Green came into the drawing-room, the Countess told him that she had overheard every word of the conversation. Dr. Green was very sorry. He saw that the nerves of the Countess were giving way. He rushed to the surgery and thence came out with a glass of some kind of liquid, which he asked the Countess to drink. "One patient is all that we can look after tonight," he said.

The Countess drank the liquid and felt that strength was coming back to her.

Dr. Green then withdrew saying he would be back in a minute, but it was full five minutes before he returned. He then asked the Countess to follow him.

They went to the surgery where Dr. Green introduced her to Dr. Crawford. Then they went to another room which was nearly dark, and stretched on a bed lay his lordship with bandages all around his face which was very little visible. Dr. Crawford went to the bed and looked at the patient. "Green," he said, "a little more light."

Dr. Green switched on the light, and Dr. Crawford after fumbling about the patient for some time announced in a hoarse whisper that the worst had happened.

The Countess had been detained a little distance from the bed. As soon as she heard the announcement of Dr. Crawford, she felt the earth slipping away from under her feet and in five seconds she was lying in a dead faint on a well-carpeted floor. Dr. Green went out and returned with the hypodermic syringe and gave an injection on the arm of the lady. He then called the well-dressed footman, and the three carried the lady to the motor car inside which she was carefully placed. Dr. Green sat inside to hold her ladyship so that she may not slide down from the seat. Dr. Crawford sat outside by the chauffeur. They soon reached the Earl's town residence, where Dr. Crawford got down and rang the bell. The footman who opened the door was informed that her ladyship had met with a nasty accident, and was unconscious. Her ladyship's maid was summoned and the two doctors with the assistance of the maid carried the unconscious form of her ladyship to her bedroom on the first floor. Her ladyship was placed on the bed, the lights were switched on, and the maid was sent for some warm water and brandy. The water and the brandy soon arrived, and a mixture of the two was with some difficulty poured down her ladyship's throat by the two doctors. "She will be all right in a few minutes," said the doctors to the maid, "and you need not be anxious; let her have perfect rest and don't undress her."

"We are both doctors, and we shall wait till the Earl arrives," said Dr. Green.

"But you forget that we have a consultation elsewhere," said Dr. Crawford.

"Yes, I am afraid we must go," said Dr. Green.

He called the footman, told him that there was no cause of alarm, and asked him to send for the family doctor. Then they both left promising that they would look her ladyship up in the morning. When the family doctor arrived, he found that there was nothing the matter with her ladyship. "It is only nerves," he said. He asked the maid to undress her, and when he was told that brandy had already been administered, he said that he need do nothing more. "She will be alright in the morning."

When the Countess recovered consciousness, she found that she was lying on her own bed. Slowly she remembered everything and wept. Finally she fell into a peaceful slumber.

When she awoke, she found her maid by her bedside. She got up sadly and began to dress.

"Where is your necklace, my lady?" asked the maid.

"I don't know and I don't care, Mary," said the Countess. "Don't talk so loudly, it jars upon my ears."

The discreet Mary kept quiet.

Slowly and sadly Lady Newford went downstairs. But think of her amazement when she saw her husband waiting for her as merry as ever.

"How do you feel this morning, Nora, my dear," was his lordship's cheerful greeting.

"You—here—you—George—they told me—"

"What did they tell you?"

"That you had an accident and were badly hurt—in fact, I went to Dr. Green's house and saw—"

With some difficulty she told her husband what she had seen and heard. His lordship was greatly puzzled. He sat deep in thought for a time and then said, "I think I can explain; what actually happened must have been this. Dr. Green saw the motor smash, the chauffeur was dead, the other man was badly injured, he thought it was I, and so he told you all that; in fact, you too thought it was myself."

"Yes, it must be that," said the Countess. "He promised to come again this morning you said?" asked her ladyship.

"So Thomas tells me."

It was afternoon and still neither Dr. Green nor Dr. Crawford turned up. Mary again mentioned the fact that the necklace was missing, but the Countess thought that it must have dropped somewhere in Dr. Green's house and that he would bring it.

At dinner the Countess mentioned the fact of the necklace to the Earl and the latter agreed with her that Dr. Green would bring it when he comes. The fact that Dr. Green did not come did not create any uneasiness, as everybody knew that he was a very busy man. The Earl, however, wrote a letter to Dr. Green and thanked him for what he had done and dropped a gentle hint about the necklace, which must have dropped at his house in the room where the patient was, and where her ladyship had fainted or in the motor car which she had been brought home.

The next day in the afternoon the doctor was announced, and his Lordship received him in the drawing-room.

"Your letter was a surprise, my lord," said the doctor after the ordinary greetings. "You say your wife—the Countess, I mean, went to my house; I am afraid you are making a mistake. "

"Yes, Dr. Green, my wife says she was taken to your place by yourself from the ball of the Countess of Sutherland and—"

"I am afraid her ladyship is making a mistake."

"You do not say there are two Doctors in London called Green."

"Not that I know of," said the medical man.

It was at this moment that the Countess came to the drawing room, and was introduced to Dr. Green. "You know Dr. Green, Nora," said his Lordship.

"Dr. Green," said the surprised lady, "but that was another gentleman, though he looked very like you."

After a few minutes of further conversation it became plain that the whole affair was a clever trick, by means of which the robbers had succeeded in procuring the famous Newford diamonds. The police were informed, and true descriptions of the two fake doctors, the footman and the chauffeur, were given, but though it is over ten years now, neither the diamonds nor the thieves have been traced.

The following were the proceedings of the special meeting of the Directors of the firm of Messrs. Hornby, Hunter & Co., held on the 1st July, 1902.

Proposed, seconded and unanimously agreed to, that the following accounts be passed:—

INCOME.

Carried over	..	..	..	..	£	100 0 0
Received in fees	..	..	..	..	£	43,000 0 0
			Total	..	£	43,100 0 0

EXPENDITURE.

Rent of a furnished flat for quarter ending 30th June		..	£	20 0 0
Rent of a furnished house for quarter ending 30th June		..	£	80 0 0
To hire of motor cars	..	..	..	..	£	9 0 0
„ cost of telegrams	..	..	..	..	£	3 0 0
Paid to each partner £ 30, per month	..	..	..	£	450 0 0
To rent of Office in advance	..	..	..	..	£	20 0 0
„ price of two motor cars	..	..	..	..	£	1,000 0 0
„ price of five bicycles	..	..	..	..	£	50 0 0
			Total	..	£	1,632 0 0

Divided among five shareholders	..	..	..	£	40,000 0 0
Balance carried over for next quarter	..	..	..	£	1,468 0 0

The managing director Dr. Hornby then delivered the following speech:—

"Gentlemen,—It is a matter for congratulation that the working of the first quarter has been so satisfactory. This shows that unity is strength not only in precept but also in practice. Gentlemen, the nine days' wonder caused by the disappearance of the Countess of Newford's diamonds has subsided, and nobody has the least idea of who the perpetrators of the offence were. As a matter of fact, gentlemen, I had the pleasure of meeting the Countess once; but, gentlemen, she did not recognise in thin, slim Dr. Hunter, the superfatted, overdressed Dr. Green of that memorable night. Gentlemen, we started this firm with the idea of collecting a capital, which will allow us to lead pious lives in future. According to our original scheme we dissolve this partnership as soon as we have got £40,000 each. At this rate, gentlemen, the £200,000 that we require will not be long in coming; but, gentlemen, we should not try luck too hard. I shall impress upon you that the robbery of the Newford diamonds has made all owners of costly diamond necklaces very suspicious. Our next transaction must be in some other line. We have been very busy of late, gentlemen, but now after all the accounts are settled we can have a little rest. But, gentlemen, we should not be extravagant. The £8,000 that each of us gets goes to the bank, and we must help ourselves as best as we can with the £30 per month. I have therefore decided, gentlemen, that we go to the seaside for a month. We shall take a house of our own, and there we shall decide what our next business will be. The expenses including the expenses of one motor car, gentlemen, will be paid out of the working capital of £1,468. I have, in anticipation of your sanction, gentlemen, taken a neat little house at Yarmouth, where a motor car has been sent, a chauffeur, a real chauffeur, has been engaged, besides a gardener, a footman and a butler. I shall be the host, gentlemen, and you will be my guests. I shall start this night, and you will all join me in three days. I now terminate the proceedings and dissolve this meeting."

Three minutes later five well-dressed, well-groomed gentlemen were seen leaving the flat.

II.—THE PICTURES.

THE house which was taken by Dr. Hunter, now temporarily called Mr. Howard, was a large one with a big compound and a spacious garden attached to it. It was one of the best houses at Yarmouth and no men of moderate means could take it because though the rent was not so very high yet the cost of keeping the garden was beyond the means of the ordinary man. The gardener was attached to the house and so were the footman and the butler and the cook. The chauffeur only had come from London. The butler was an old man who had been in Yarmouth all his life and he could say everything about every house in the place. The footman was some relation of the butler and he too was well informed.

Three days after Mr. Howard's arrival came his four guests. The servants who are still attached to the house will tell you that they were five jolly old, confirmed bachelors. They were an over-merry, careless lot who all the time that they were at Merriville (that was the designation of the house) ate, drank and made themselves merry. They were out most of the time, kept no regular hours and played bridge when the weather kept them indoors. Old Mr. Howard with a slight hump, which his guests called his scholarly stoop, was the easiest going of all masters. He did everything for himself, specially his dressing, in which he never sought the aid of the footman. Why he had not brought his own footman from London, neither John Smith the butler nor Thomas Hardy the footman ever understood.

The master, Mr. Howard, always liked late dinners and the guests were even more tardy. They never sat down to dinner till well after nine at night and kept on smoking and chatting till midnight. But the servants were allowed to retire soon after 10.30.

At the dinner table they discussed England and America, bicycles and motor cars, watches and necklaces and all sorts of things, and from their conversation it was evident to the servants that like their master, Mr. Howard, his guests were all shrewd business men and enormously rich. They were all good-tempered people and made friendship fast. Within a month of their arrival their roll of acquaintances had swelled enormously and there were a number of neat little dinner parties which the richest and best people of the neighbourhood joined with pleasure. Within six weeks of their arrival they had become the most talked-of people in the whole neighbourhood.

On the 10th of August, after the servants had retired to rest, Mr. Howard and his guests were sitting at the dinner table with wines and cigars, and a lively discussion was going on.

"The three Corots* at Leonard Villa ought to sell for £12,000," said Mr. Howard.

"Undoubtedly they will, did you not hear old Johnson say that he purchased them for £18,000 and was offered £20,000," said Mr. Little.

"How long shall we have to keep them before we can sell them out without fear—?" asked Mr. Rider.

"If we ship them off to America, we can find a purchaser without difficulty who will pay fair price and ask no questions," said Mr. Carman.

"But how will you avoid the custom officer?" asked Mr. Howard.

"That will be my business," said Mr. Carman. "You procure the pictures for me and—"

They all agreed that Mr. Carman would have to go to America with the pictures, but then it was discovered that Mr. Rider knew more people in New York who would purchase things without asking questions than Mr. Carman did. But Mr. Rider would not undertake to avoid the custom barrier safely. It was, therefore, decided that both Mr. Rider and Mr. Carman should go. The expenses would be high, but that could not be helped. Moreover, some such accident may happen that it may require two brains to bridge over any temporary difficulty.

---

* Jean-Baptiste-Camille Corot (1796–1875): French landscape and portrait painter.

There was a large gathering of ladies and gentlemen at the house of Mr. Johnson, the millionaire, of Leonard Villa. The dinner was to be followed by a dance and at dinner the engagement of Emily Johnson with the impecunious Lord Hallbury was to be announced. This gentleman had inherited an empty title and a bare £500 per year which scarcely kept him in cigars, and so there it was that the rich heiress Emily Johnson came in handy. It was a marriage more for convenience than love and everybody at Yarmouth knew it. Lord Hallbury and Emily Johnson were the two special favourites of old Mr. Howard of the Scholarly Stoop and the engagement ring that was to be given to Emily that night was a present from the last named gentleman to Lord Hallbury. It was a costly ring with a single diamond in it and must have cost at least £400. Besides the ring Mr. Howard had promised Emily a diamond necklace worth £2,000 on her wedding day that was not very far off. After dinner, in the usual course of things, the engagement was announced and the date fixed for the marriage was also made known. The wedding was to take place early in November.

The dance commenced at about ten and all the fairest and best joined. Mr. Howard had quietly slipped away, but as everybody else was engaged none took any notice of the fact.

Mr. Howard quietly slipped out of the hot ball-room, went into the dining-room and thence into Mr. Johnson's office which was in darkness. He groped his way about, opened the communication door* and passed into the corridor. Quietly and silently like a cat he passed through it and reached the door of the picture gallery. The door was securely locked. Mr. Howard produced the key which Mr. Hunter had given him earlier in the day and with a trembling hand inserted it into the lock and turned it. The lock opened with a click. Mr. Howard looked fearfully around. The corridor was in total darkness, as while coming along he had switched off the only electric light. Nobody had overheard. He passed into the room the walls of which were literally covered with costly pictures. He then closed the door behind him and felt for the switch. Soon the room was flooded with light. Mr. Howard, all nervousness now gone, walked straight to where the three Corots were. He took out a sharp knife from his pocket, took down each picture in turn and removed it neatly from the frame. He then rolled up the pictures, wrapped up the lot in a sheet of newspaper, opened the window and dropped the pictures through the bars on the lawn below: He then closed the window, put out the light and came to the door. He listened for

---

* Double doors in one frame that can be opened from either side for privacy.

half a minute. Everything was silent as death. He turned the handle but the door would not yield. Mr. Howard had forgotten to remove the key from the lock outside and bring it along with him. Somebody must have observed him, after all, then. He was trapped like a rat. He stood inside with clenched fists and clattering teeth. It meant an exposure and probably a trial. It meant the failure of all his schemes and probably there months in jail. He stood inert for full one minute, then he heard the key turned in the lock. He knew that everything was over but he could not stir an inch. The door slowly opened. The corridor lamp was alight. Mr. Howard heaved a sigh of great relief. It was only Mr. Hunter. "You are a fool, Hornby," said Mr. Hunter. "You had no business to leave the key outside. I thought I would give you a lesson."

"Has anybody observed my absence?" asked Mr. Howard.

"Nobody yet, but if you stand there trembling like a coward, I am sure somebody will," said Mr. Hunter sternly.

Mr. Howard came out but he was trembling still. Softly they went out of the corridor after taking care that the key had not been left in the lock this time. Then they entered the darkened office and by way of the conservatory returned to the dining-room which had been converted into a supper-room with a number of small tables. They sat down at one of the tables and Mr. Hunter ordered whisky. "Drink it, it will help to restore your nerves to order," laughed Mr. Hunter. "I shall in the meantime go and see that the pictures are safely concealed in the motor car."

While Mr. Howard was still sipping his whisky, Miss Ethel Cotwood came in.

"You here, Mr. Howard, I thought you were dancing," said Miss Cotwood.

"I thought I should have a drink first and a cigar afterwards," smiled Mr. Howard.

"On the lawn? Don't you think this room too hot," asked Miss Cotwood.

Mr. Howard again felt his nerves leaving him, but it would not do to give way; Hunter must be given five clear minutes to stow away the pictures safely.

"Are you not dancing," he asked.

"No, I shall have a stroll first, on the lawn, and that with you," smiled Miss Cotwood.

"Then you must wait for two minutes, and let me finish my drink." Miss Cotwood agreed.

Mr. Howard did not approve of drinking whisky after dinner, but he did order another glass and sat sipping. Hunter must have his five minutes. Before he had finished his glass, however, Hunter returned all radiant. From his face Mr. Howard knew that everything was all right.

"You are not dancing, Hunter," asked Mr. Howard.

"I may ask you the same question," replied Mr. Hunter.

"We are going out for a stroll on the lawn first," said Miss Cotwood.

Mr. Howard had in the meantime finished his drink and lighted a cigar. Miss Cotwood dragged him away, leaving Mr. Hunter lighting another cigarette.

Old Mr. Howard was a universal favourite. His Daimler Landaulet was used more by the *children of Yarmouth*, as he called them, than by himself. His age and his wealth, moreover, gave him a privilege which few men enjoyed. He called every young girl his darling, and every young man his young friend. Within a month of his arrival at Yarmouth he could say a lot of things about people more than anybody else. Confidential family matters had been discussed with him which none except the members knew.

"What do you think about the engagement of Emily, Mr. Howard?" asked Miss Cotwood.

"I don't think of things that do not concern me directly," said Mr. Howard.

"But Emily is your darling."

"So are you, my dear."

"But do you think she will be happy," asked Miss Cotwood.

"I have no reason to think otherwise," replied Mr. Howard sagely.

"But Emily does not love him."

"She will be dutiful and he will be kind and loving."

"Then you approve."

"Of course I do."

"Did you know him before?"

"Never met him till he came here."

"Then how can you say he will be kind and loving,"

"I can read the character of a man on his face," said Mr. Howard.

"Then do read my character, please."

"I said I could read the character of a man."

"Oh, Mr. Howard, you are—"

"Yes, fire away, my dear, I am—"

"You are—you are absurd."

"But not stupid."

"You are intolerable, let us go in."

"I don't mind."

As they went in, Miss Cotwood left Mr. Howard and joined a group of youngsters. Mr. Howard was subsequently joined by Emily Johnson.

"Why are you looking so pensive, Emily?" asked Mr. Howard.

"Oh, let us go out, Mr. Howard, the room is so hot and I want to speak to you," said Emily with a sigh. "Do you think, Mr. Howard, that—that—"

"Yes I think you will be very happy," said Mr. Howard, guessing what was forthcoming. "Lord Hallbury is not a man who will make his wife unhappy."

"But you see, he cares more for my money than for myself."

"In three months you will find the order of things reversed," said Mr. Howard sapiently.

"Do you really think so?"

"I am sure of it."

"But I hardly know him."

"Look here, Emily, my dear, you must not forget that your father knows things much better than you do. You have heard about love and have read a lot about it in novels, but it is all rot. No novelist knows what true love is. Your father and myself are not very old friends, it is true, but we are good friends. He had consulted me and I had agreed with him and we both think it is a very good match."

"But I hardly know him. "

"But we do; you must remember that whatever your father does is for your good and I have no reason to do otherwise. "

They then went inside.

"Where have you been, Howard," asked Mr. Johnson, as they went inside. "I have hardly seen your face since the dancing commenced. "

"Out on the lawn all the time with some young girl or other," said Mr. Howard imperturbably.

"Yes, you would not dance, and not allow Miss Cotwood—"

"It was Miss Cotwood who suggested that I should go out with her," interposed Mr. Howard with a smile.

"Come and let us have a drink. Your friends are all dancing and I am always happy when I see youngsters enjoy," said Mr. Johnson.

The dance lasted till four in the morning and they all enjoyed themselves immensely. The stars were fading in the east when our five friends went to bed.

The next day there was the following conversation after dinner, after the servants had retired to rest at Merriville.

"How did you procure the key, Hunter," asked Mr. Howard.

"I would bet you a penny, you can't guess," smiled Mr. Hunter triumphantly.

"No, we are afraid we can't."

"Then I shall tell you," said Mr. Hunter helping himself to some whisky. "You know I always maintain that it is a very foolish thing to leave the key behind in the lock when you are going inside a room and will stay there for some time."

"Yes, you always say that, in fact you gave me the greatest shock I ever had in my life last night, when you locked the door from outside," said Mr. Howard, the very memory of which situation set him trembling.

"Well, it was like this," continued Mr. Hunter. "The day that old Johnson took us to see the pictures 1 knew that I should require the key, so I had taken with me a ball of well-kneaded flour. As you all went in, you must have observed that I brushed against the key and it dropped from the lock. I picked it up and reinserted it. Old Johnson was at that time busy with opening the windows on the other side of the room. But before I restored the key to the luck, I took a neat impression of it on the ball of flour."

"But why flour, why not wax," asked Mr. Carman.

"My dear Carman, wax is something very old. I wanted to do it on original lines; moreover wax leaves the key oily."

"Well, proceed," said Mr. Howard.

"There is not much to add. I had been a jeweller's assistant long enough, and nothing was easier than making a key like that," said Mr. Hunter helping himself to a little port.

"I wonder when he will discover the theft," said Mr. Rider.

"Not before the beginning of the next season when some guests come in, or probably on the occasion of his daughter's marriage," said Mr. Howard.

"By that time the pictures will have been sold and the money realised," said Mr. Hunter.

"If luck does not desert us."

"When does the next boat for America sail?" asked Mr. Hunter.

"On the day after tomorrow, and we go by that," said Mr. Carman. "My servant Rider and myself."

The voyage from Liverpool to New York was the pleasantest Mr. Carman had ever enjoyed. Posing as a Cotton King he found himself the most important man on the steamer. His servant Rider was equally important among the steerage passengers.

Mr. Carman could talk a good deal on any subject, but motor cars seemed to be his favourite theme. It was understood that he had purchased the best motor car in England, that the King of England once drove in that car and Mr. Carman sat behind the wheel himself and went so fast that His Majesty had palpitation of heart and the policeman stopped them. "You should have seen the officer's face when he discovered who my fellow motorist was," was Mr. Carman's favourite remark.

"You should see my master's new motor," Mr. Carman's servant would say to his fellow voyagers. "It would do your heart good to have a look at the thing."

The voyage came to an end uneventfully. As each voyager passed through the customs barrier, he or she was critically examined.

Mr. Carman's turn came. The officers saw a stout gentleman, stiff and straight as if he had swallowed a poker, with an enormous gold chain from which dangled a masonic charm set with diamonds. They allowed him to pass.

"My servant will show you that there is nothing dutiable with me," said Mr. Carman in his lordly style.

"Thank you, Sir," said the Yankee who could not for the life of him guess that the real size of the gentleman before him was seven inches smaller round the waist and that the padding contained three rolled up pictures which were very much dutiable.

Seventeen days after the theft of the pictures from Mr. Johnson's house, Mr. Howard one morning received the following telegram from America.

"14,150 bags safely arrived, approved, returning Corona Tuesday." Mr. Howard was at his breakfast with his two guests. The telegram was handed over to him. He read it and passed it on with a smile to his guests.

"Not a bad business after all," said Mr. Hunter.

Three days after the receipt of this mysterious telegram all Yarmouth knew that Mr. Howard with the scholarly stoop and the motor car was a corn merchant who sent bags to America. And they were all satisfied inasmuch as everybody wants to know the affairs of his neighbours in spite of the fact that he looks indifferent.

By the time Messrs. Carman and Rider returned, all the people knew or supposed they knew everything about the mysterious residents of Merriville.

It was about the end of October that one morning our friends were sitting at breakfast which was nearly over, but Mr. Howard and his guests were still sitting at the table. One of them was reading the morning paper and the others were listening. Miss Johnson was announced.

"Show her into the drawing-room," said Mr. Howard.

But Emily Johnson, whose friendship with Mr. Howard had continuously increased, came into the dining-room which was adjacent to the drawing-room, without any ceremony and dropped into a chair. She was breathless and flushed.

"Early rising and a brisk walk has done you good, Emily, my dear," said Mr. Howard peering over his gold framed glasses. He was not reading but he had reading glasses on.

"Oh Mr. Howard—there has been a theft in the house and all the pictures have gone," panted Emily.

Mr. Little who was reading the paper, put it down on the table and then all of them looked at Emily and then at each other.

"You don't mean to say that the thief has carted away all the pictures—there were about four hundred of them," said Mr. Howard.

"No, the three Corots have gone."

"Where," asked Mr. Little.

"That is exactly what we do not know," said Emily.

"The three Corots gone," said Mr. Howard slowly. "They were the best of the lot."

"They were, and father is mad with rage and grief," said Emily.

"When were they stolen—last night?" asked Mr. Carman.

"That is what we do not know," said Emily. "The rooms were opened after how long we do not remember."

"But why were the rooms opened?" asked Mr. Howard.

"There were some guests and they wanted to see the pictures," said Emily. "Father keeps the keys himself."

"Well—" said Mr. Howard.

"We went in this morning and discovered that the pictures were gone."

"Did you find any of the windows open—or—"

"No, everything was just as father had left it when he went in last, that was about two months ago."

"Does Johnson suspect anybody," asked Mr. Howard.

"How can he, did I not tell you that he is too angry and prostrated with grief," said Emily.

"Smith," shouted Mr. Howard, "the car at once."

"I go on my bicycle," said Mr. Rider.

"I walk with Little," said Mr. Hunter, and the three gentlemen marched out of the room.

"Have the police been informed," asked Mr. Carman.

"Not so long as I was there," said Emily.

"Then as we go we shall pick up Inspector Hickman on the way," said Mr. Howard. "Have a cup of coffee in the meantime, Emily, my dear."

"Thanks, I think I do require a drink."

The coffee came and our friends sat silent till Emily had finished it. The car was ready in the meantime and they all started. Mr. Howard's chauffeur was a clever man, and could drive fast. Within five minutes of starting they had reached the police station where Mr. Howard informed Mr. Hickman that there had been a theft at Mr. Johnson's house. The inspector was ready to go with them in three minutes and by the time Messrs. Little and Hunter had arrived, Mr. Howard reached Mr. Johnson's house in his car. Everything was in a confusion there. Four guests had arrived on the previous evening for Miss Johnson's wedding and it was to show them the pictures that the rooms had been opened that morning after breakfast when the theft was discovered. Everybody had a theory of his own, but neither Mr. Johnson nor Mr. Hickman could find any clue of the thief. The windows were just as Mr. Johnson had left them on the occasion of his last visit and the door lock, which was a costly Chubb's key-catcher*, had not been tampered with. The pictures had simply vanished. Mr. Johnson was simply prostrated with grief. He used to be so proud of his Corots. The rooms were never dusted except in the presence of the owner and so if there were any marks left on the dust on the carpet, they had vanished before the arrival of Hickman, so many people had gone in since the morning.

Mr. Porter, one of the guests, thought it was one of the servants who had a duplicate key. Mr. Leslie, another guest, thought it was a clever thief, but how the clever thief got away without being detected was the puzzle.

"It was a thief, since he has stolen the pictures," said Mr. Howard sagely, "and he is very clever since he has left no trace behind, but that does not help us very much."

Everybody agreed.

After a lot of discussion it was decided that a private detective should be engaged to trace the pictures as well as the thief. It is over ten years now but neither the pictures nor the thief has been discovered. Mr. Johnson agrees with everybody else that it was a very clever thief.

---

* A type of lock with a safety mechanism that jams if anything other than the exact key is used (i.e. frustrating lock picking tools). Chubb locks are popularly used in fiction (especially Victorian-era mysteries) as locks that are "unable to be picked."

The following were the proceedings of the special meeting of the Directors of the firm of Messrs. Hornby, Hunter & Co., held on the 30th November, 1902.

Proposed, seconded and unanimously agreed to, that the following accounts be passed:—

INCOME.

Carried over from last quarter	..	..	..	£	1,468 0 0
By sale of pictures	..	..	..	£	14,150 0 0
		Total	..	£	15,618 0 0

EXPENDITURE.

House at Yarmouth	..	..	..	£	340 0 0
One gold ring for Lord Hallbury	..	..	..	£	240 0 0
One diamond necklace for Emily	..	..	..	£	1,400 0 0
Expenses at Yarmouth	..	..	..	£	1,500 0 0
Trip to America	..	..	..	£	128 0 0
Expenses in America	..	..	..	£	20 0 0
Rent of furnished flat in London for quarter ending 31st December, 1902*	..	..	..	£	20 0 0
Other miscellaneous expenses	..	..	..	£	100 0 0
		Total	..	£	3,748 0 0

Paid to shareholders £2,000 each	..	..	..	£	10,000 0 0
Carried forward for next quarter	..	..	..	£	1,870 0 0

The Chairman, Dr. Hornby, then made the following speech:—"Gentlemen I am glad to be back in London. When at Yarmouth I took good care that everybody should know that I was a corn merchant who sent bags to America. After all, gentlemen, I fail to see why we should not be corn merchants. After we have sufficient capital accumulated, I intend to start a firm of corn importers. We require £150,000 more. By the help of you all, gentlemen, I expect the money will be found and then goodbye to our

---

* Corrected in this edition from "December, 1912," an obvious typographical error.

present business. Let us hope that day will soon come. After that if our profits allow, we shall pay off all our constituents, including the Countess of Newford.

I now intend to take a house in Harley Street and treat the American millionaire, and get as much out of him as I possibly can. You, gentlemen, will have to be my trusted and devoted servants, because the game will be rather risky and I dare not engage any servants. But I shall be a kind master. Today we part, gentlemen, to meet again this day week in my Harley Street house. 1 declare the proceedings closed and this meeting dissolved."

III.—THE DOCTOR.

THESE were the circumstances under which our friends met next.

Dr. Hornby called himself Dr. Newman and as such he took a house in Harley Street. It was given out that he was a medical practitioner from India and that there he had learnt some special kinds of Indian cures for some complaints which the British medical science had no idea about. For instance, he knew some particularly potent Indian cures for nervous troubles which no English doctor knew anything of. He had his own dispensary from which he dispensed his medicines and wrote his prescriptions in a language which was not intelligible to the ordinary chemists. Mr. Hunter, now called Mr. Sportsman, was his laboratory assistant and he was the only man who could read Dr. Newman's prescriptions.

Dr. Newman began to get patients. Soon after he began practice in London he found that he was getting on.

Of course he was a real medical man, and a very clever one too, and in some cases he did cure people whom the great London specialists had given up as hopeless. The reason was that in many cases, and specially in cases of nervous trouble, faith had a good deal to do with cures; and Dr. Newman's patients had faith in him. The reason thereof will be explained later on. The very fact that he had a wide Indian experience and knew some potent Indian cures which none but the Indian *Kavirajas* (Hindu doctors) or *Unani Hakims* (Muhammadan physicians) knew, attracted a great many people. The fact that he knew no more about Indian medicines than he knew about the man in the moon, did not stand in his way at all.

Dr. Newman went on in grand style, for he knew that he could not practise for more than six months and there were enough people in London to keep him going for that period. Moreover, he had over £1,800 belonging to the firm of Messrs. Hornby, Hunter & Co.

The American multi-millionaire had to be fleeced and as soon as that was done, they would hasten to fresh fields and pastures new. That was the plan. The few patients that came found that the doctor had a roaring practice. He was out nearly all day and never came when he was asked to—and pleaded pressure of work.

Lady Newton was one of the first patients that the Doctor had. She had seen his advertisements and came to consult him. He at once saw that there was nothing the matter with her. So he told her that he must see her for at least a month to study the symptoms and prescribe Indian medicines. Her ladyship was only too pleased. The next morning she sent the doctor a cheque for £150 in full payment of his fees for one month in advance for his daily visits. The doctor called on her the next day and stayed for full one hour talking on all sorts of subjects.

"I shall observe all your ladyship's symptoms while I talk," said the doctor, "and then I shall prescribe for you some medicine which no British medical man has dreamt of."

"I am sure you will be able to cure me, doctor," said Lady Newton. "Something here tells me that," and she placed her hand on her heart.

The doctor came away after an hour, leaving her ladyship exceedingly pleased with him and with herself.

That night Dr. Newman had the following conversation with his chauffeur Mr. Carman, now called Mr. Runner.

"Have you found out many things, Carman," asked the Doctor.

"Nothing beyond the fact that her ladyship has got an English maid who is very garrulous."

"Then I am sure you will be able to find out everything in a day or two."

"I hope so, Sir," said Mr. Runner. "If it will help you, you may as well know now that her ladyship takes no milk in her tea."

"And sugar?"

"No sugar either."

"Anything else?"

"I shall be able to tell you something more tomorrow," said Mr. Runner.

"Thanks, if you could handle the maid properly, I shall be able to tackle her ladyship properly," smiled Dr. Newman.

When Dr. Newman went to see her Ladyship the next day, she asked him if he would have a cup of tea. The Doctor readily consented and in a most matter of fact way asked whether her ladyship disliked sugar and milk.

"I hate sugar and milk," said her ladyship.

"I thought as much," said the doctor.

"Why," asked Lady Newton.

"Because," said the doctor," I am afraid you are suffering from *Ghore Ambashtha Mrigi*, and one of the chief symptoms of that disease is that the patient does not like milk and sugar."

"Is that an Indian disease?" asked Lady Newton anxiously.

"It is not exactly an Indian disease, but it is a disease which the British doctors have no idea about."

"Is it dangerous?" asked her ladyship.

"Not at all, only incurable by English doctors."

"Then you are sure I have got it."

"Not yet, I must keep you under observation for some time."

"Then supposing I have got it, you will be able to cure me."

"Oh, certainly, if that is what you have really got, seven days of Kaviraji treatment will bring you round," said the doctor.

The next day the doctor came again and one of the first things he did was to take her ladyship's hands and examine them carefully.

"You get your nails manicured every day," asked the doctor.

"Yes, long nails—"

"Give you something like a nervous shock." It was the doctor who completed the sentence.

"And you want your chauffeur to drive very slow," continued the doctor. "You cannot stand speed."

"Fast driving gives me a headache and I feel giddy afterwards," said Lady Newton.

That evening after dinner the doctor sent for his chauffeur Mr. Runner, better known as Mr. Carman, and Mr. Sportsman, formerly known to us as Mr. Hunter, Mr. Little, now called Smith (the butler) and Mr. Rider, now called Mr. Jones (the footman) were of course there.

"We are going on exceedingly well, Carman," said the doctor. "You go on making love to that silly fool of her Ladyship's maid and in ten days we shall have the entire six months rent out of her ladyship."

"But go very slowly and see that nobody suspects anything," put in Mr. Hunter.

"Ask her whether Lady Newton likes company at dinner or she prefers to be alone with her husband," said the Doctor.

"All right, Sir—" said Mr. Carman with mock humility.

And they all laughed.

It was a week after the aforesaid conversation. The Doctor was certain that it was *Ghore Ambashtha Mrigi.* The symptoms of this nervous disorder the doctor described with such wonderful accuracy that her Ladyship thought that he had been specially sent by God to cure her. Naturally the costly Kaviraji medicines which the Doctor prescribed did her Ladyship much good. After a complete cure which took about a month, she was gratified to receive the following letter from the Doctor in reply to the one she had sent him.

"My dear Lady Newton,—The cheque for £1,000 was duly received, for which accept many thanks. I am really happy that I have been able to cure you. Allow me to assure you that here was nothing wonderful about my treatment. The disease that you had is not so very uncommon in India. Nearly all the Hindu physicians know the cure. How I wish some of our so-called London Specialists would go to India to learn from the Hindus some of their methods of Nerve Cure, etc., etc., etc."

It was about the middle of March that the American multi-millionaire, after having tried nearly all the London Specialists, came to Dr. Newman for advice. His trouble was sleeplessness. He could not sleep soundly, and when he did sleep he was always troubled with terrible dreams. Probably it was Lady Newton's cure, that had been so much talked about in London, that induced Mr. Richmond to seek the advice of Dr. Newman.

He found the Doctor a tall stout gentleman of about fifty-five, with close-cut grey hair and tanned skin.

"Thirty years in India has bleached my hair and tanned my skin," said Dr. Newman with a smile.

The American was impressed. He had heard about the cure of Lady Newton. It was arranged that Dr. Newman would pay him a visit every day for a month to observe his symptoms and then prescribe some Indian medicine if he found that the diagnosis was correct. A cheque for £120 was handed over at once and it was settled that £20,000 would be paid if a complete cure was effected.

The doctor used to be very punctual. He went to the residence of Mr. Richmond every day after lunch and stayed for an hour. "You should not tell me anything," said Dr. Newman to Mr. Richmond on the occasion of his first visit. "I shall find out everything myself."

It was after the doctor had been paying his regular visits for over a fortnight that he explained one day to Mr. Richmond that when a man hates motor cars, and likes to take four spoonfuls of sugar in his tea, and an ounce of lime juice in his glass of whiskey and prefers an extra hot bath, and whenever he sits for some time with his legs on the table and goes to sleep, and puts an extra spoonful of salt in his soup, etc., etc., the Hindu medical science called his sleeplessness *Ashaktic Anidra*.

He further assured his patient that no British medical man who did not know Indian medicine could cure him.

Mr. Richmond was really surprised. The symptoms so much tallied with his own.

"If the Indian medical science is so perfect, Doctor," said he, "what do all these Europeans go there for?"

"They go there to fleece the Nabobs* and the educated fools," suggested the doctor sagely. "Moreover, there is no surgery in the Indian medical science."

"But the symptoms seem to have been described with wonderful accuracy," said Mr. Richmond.

"There are many wonderful things in India of which Europe has no idea," said Dr. Newman.

Naturally Mr. Richmond began using the medicines prescribed by Dr. Newman with great zeal.

A month passed, but the Ayurvedic medicine did not do Mr. Richmond much good. The doctor told Mr. Richmond that the cure would take fully three months, and therefore the latter was not uneasy. But the doctor was. He had been promised £20,000 if he could bring about a cure, and the chances of getting that sum honestly was growing smaller and smaller every day. The £5 that the doctor received for his daily visits was certainly not enough for his Harley Street establishment. The £1,000 of Lady Newton had come very handy, but to hoodwink a shrewd American was a different matter altogether. It was very easy to tell the symptoms of *Ashaktic Anidra* by the help of Mr. Carman, but to cure a disease in which the great London specialists had failed was well, you can guess. By the beginning of May the doctor became desperate; he found that the £20,000 were not for him unless he got it by some means which were not quite professional. So a council of war was called to decide what steps should be taken. Unless something was done within the next thirty days, £1,200 would have to be paid for house rent.

"Yes, the yachting proposal is the best," said Dr. Newman, "I think that is the least dangerous course."

---

* Person who returned from India to Europe with a fortune.

"It is the cleverest thing," suggested Mr. Rider.

"But it will be very expensive," said Mr. Little.

"We should not mind a little expense, gentlemen, if the thing is safe enough," said the doctor. "I do not believe in the penny-wise-pound-foolish sort of way of working."

"Exactly," said Mr. Hunter, "nobody at Yarmouth will ever guess that Mr. Howard with the scholarly—"

"Stop, I say," shouted Dr. Newman, "we should not waste time. I shall suggest the sea-trip to him tomorrow."

"By the way, Hornby," said Mr. Hunter, "what is *Ashaktic*?"

"I have not got the least idea," admitted Mr. Hornby with a smile.

"But where did you learn the word?"

"From an Indian dictionary."

"But what does it actually mean apart from *Anidra*?"

"That I really forget."

"A most dangerous thing to do. Suppose he meets an Indian, there are so many here, and asks."

"No fear of that," said Dr. Newman. "He will not be able to pronounce the word properly and the Indian will not understand."

The next day Dr. Newman suggested to Mr. Richmond that a short sea-trip towards the north would do him good.

Mr. Richmond consented, but he consented only on the condition that the doctor himself would go with him.

After great hesitation Dr. Newman consented to go, but on condition that he was paid £1,000 before he started, to remunerate him to a certain extent for the loss that his practice would suffer from his absence.

The money was paid and the doctor, with the assistance of Mr. Grenville, the American's private secretary, selected a yacht and also the captain and the crew. The boat was furnished with a taste which did credit to the Doctor's sense of the beautiful and comfortable. The two state saloons were occupied by Mr. Richmond and the Doctor, the secretary had a beautiful cabin to himself and the servants were as comfortably accommodated as on any first-class liner. Mr. Richmond had brought three servants and the doctor only one, namely, Mr. Rider now called Mr. Jones, the footman of the Harley Street establishment.

The Captain was a jolly good fellow, but he spoke in a language which was to all practical purposes incomprehensible to Mr. Richmond.

Soon after they started from Portsmouth Mr. Richmond brought out a chair and invited the doctor to come and sit near him.

"I wonder, Doctor, why I never thought of yachting before," said Mr. Richmond.

"In half an hour you will say you wonder why you ever came out," laughed the Doctor.

"Oh, you mean I shall become sea-sick."

"Rather," said the doctor.

"Then you will soon find out that the sea does not affect me in the least," said Mr. Richmond. "At least the sickness does not last for any length of time."

It was a very sunny afternoon in the first week of May and Mr. Richmond was as happy as a child. So was the doctor. He had every reason to be, as will appear later on.

"Oh, Mr. Richmond does not mind the sickness at all," said Mr. Grenville the Secretary. "He has crossed the Atlantic thrice."

"I am very glad to hear it," said the doctor, "but a yacht is different from an Atlantic Liner."

The voyage was to last for a month. They went right round Land's End and Ireland and the North of Scotland to Norway and thence to Dantzig. Then they retraced their steps homewards.

At Dantzig they anchored and remained for a couple of days. The Doctor said that he would land and travel overland and join them again at Hamburg. He would have to see a German specialist about Mr. Richmond's disease, he said. He, however, left his footman behind.

"You must go very slowly," were his parting instructions, "otherwise you will have to wait for me at Hamburg. I shall have to be in Berlin for a day and I hope I shall not keep you waiting."

Mr. Richmond was not sorry to part with him. He was glad to be free. The Doctor had kept him under such strict discipline that he was getting tired of it all. So like a schoolboy he was glad to be free. He went very slowly indeed and reached Hamburg on the fifth day after leaving Dantzig, but there was no Dr. Newman in the hotel where he ought to have been. "He must have been detained in Berlin," said he to his secretary.

Dr. Newman in the meantime had reached Berlin and from there sent a telegram to Mr. Hunter enquiring how matters were progressing, and on being informed by a telegram in reply that everything was alright, instead of going over to Hamburg, had travelled to London overland and on the date that the yacht reached Hamburg he was safe in his house in Harley Street.

The day after he reached London he deposited £20,000 in the Bank of

England and then went over to live in his flat in Bloomsbury as if nothing had happened. He was Mr. Hornby once more. The Harley Street establishment, however, was not broken up.

Mr. Richmond waited for Dr. Newman at Hamburg for four days. Then he became very uneasy. Mr. Jones was also looking concerned at his master's non-appearance. Telegrams were dispatched to all sorts of places but no news about Dr. Newman was forthcoming.

With a heavy heart Mr. Richmond sailed from Hamburg and after a week reached London. He inquired about Dr. Newman at the Harley Street house but was informed that they knew nothing about the doctor's whereabouts at that place. The servants were very anxious and so was the landlord. The doctor must have met with an accident. He, however, soon understood how matters were, when he found that a cheque for £20,000 drawn in favour of the doctor had been presented at the bank and the payment received in cash gold. It was only then that Mr. Richmond scented foul play and the police were made acquainted with the facts.

They raided the house in Harley Street but found nothing to give them any clue as to the doctor's whereabouts. All the servants, including Mr. Sportsman, swore that their salaries were badly in arrears. The footman and the butler as well as the chauffeur gave minute descriptions of the doctor; the chauffeur minutely described the places where the doctor used to go but nobody knew anything about the doctor at these places. The motor car had to be sold to pay the servants, Mr. Richmond claiming nothing against the servants, and the landlord had to content himself with a few pieces of furniture which the doctor had purchased to suit his taste. After a protracted enquiry the police gave up the case as hopeless. Dr. Newman's portrait still hangs on the walls of Scotland Yard with an inscription below, that £1,000 would be paid to anybody who furnished the authorities with some clue as to the whereabouts of the gentleman whose portrait it was.

It is, however, over nine years and the reward still remains unclaimed.

The servants, with the exception of the cook, after their discharge from Harley Street, have not sought re-engagement elsewhere.

The following were the proceedings of the special meeting of the Directors of the firm of Messrs. Hornby, Hunter & Co., held on the 30th September, 1903.

Proposed, seconded and unanimously agreed to, that the following accounts be passed:—

INCOME.

Cash in hand	£	1,870 0 0
Received in fees	£	4,380 0 0
Received from Mr. Richmond, special honorarium ..	£	20,000 0 0
Total ..	£	26,250 0 0

EXPENDITURE.

Harley Street House	£	1,200 0 0
Expenses at Harley Street	£	3,000 0 0
Paid to each shareholder for miscellaneous expenses @ £100	£	500 0 0
Miscellaneous expenses	£	100 0 0
Rent of furnished flat in London for quarter ending 31st Dec., 1903	£	80 0 0
Total ..	£	4,880 0 0

Distributed among shareholders @ £4,000 each ..	£	20,000 0 0
Grand Total ..	£	24,880 0 0

Balance carried forward	£	1,370 0 0

THE END.

S. N. MUKERJI.

ALLAHABAD.

Interior illustration from *The Lady's Realm*:
"Gentleman's Club" by Howard Somerville (1907).

Interior illustration by Dakshinaranjan Mitra Majumder
from *Thakurmar Jhuli* (*Grandmother's Bag* [*of Tales*]) (1907).

WHO WAS S. MUKERJI?

S. MUKERJI was active as an author only between the years 1913–1919 in British-governed India. He first wrote the serialized *The Mysterious Traders* for publication in late 1913 (as S.N. Mukerji) and then wrote *Indian Ghost Stories* for publication the following year (1914). He seems never to have published again (at least under the name of S. Mukerji or S.N. Mukerji), yet remained in good enough standing with the publisher, A.H. Wheeler & Co., to return and pen a new preface for the second edition of *Indian Ghost Stories* in 1917 and then again a postscript for the fourth edition in 1919 (published 1921).

There is little else found factually about this author. But I can herein speculate...

Although there were many accomplished female authors of the era (M. E. <Mary Elizabeth> Braddon, Agatha Christie, Baroness <Emma> Orczy, Amelia Edwards, e.g.), S. Mukerji was almost certainly male. The protagonist of everything written by Mukerji is male, and his writing uniformly expresses a male-dominated worldview. Females in the stories are treated as romantic interests, spurned lovers, background family members, or lingering spirits. The tone of writing lacks even a sensitivity to female depth or perception; none of the female characters exhibit curiosity or courage or wisdom. It is always the male who has the answer, always the male who is the hero or intrepid investigator while women are painted as naïve or gullible, particularly in *The Mysterious Traders*.

Next is more readily apparent that S. Mukerji was an educated and literary man, filling his writings with reference to world events, governance, history, and literary quotes (notably an immoderate enthusiasm for Shakespeare). He seems the archetype of a refined, learned gentleman of his time, suggesting presumably that he attended university, which further suggests he had some—at least modest—financial means.

The occasional internet sleuth has claimed him so well educated as to be pen name of Dr. Santosh Kumar (S.K.) Mukherji, M.B., a 1920s Calcutta-based researcher and author of such medical record books as *Infantile Cirrhosis of Liver* (1922); *Elements of Endocrinology* (1924); *Prostitution in India* (1925); and *Incompatibility in Prescriptions* (1928). The assertion feels clearly implausible and given without any proof or merit except the supposed similarity of name (the surname spelled in variant with an "h," and even the "S.K." is mismatched to "S.N." as attributed to *The Mysterious Traders*). Even more unlikely to the prospect of this dual career as medical author is the next point:

S. Mukerji was almost certainly a Caucasian Englishman. Proponents of historic Asian fiction auteurs have pointed to Mukerji as example of an accomplished and diverse writer of India, either Bengali-specific or more generalized as inclusive of the broader Asian diaspora. Notably in his writings for *Indian Ghost Stories*, Mukerji himself makes frequent assurances that he was present and part of haunting experience among Indian children, college students, or government clerks, and along with his ostensible Brahmin-evocative surname leads readers to believe his voice as authentic of the culture.

In scrutiny, this seems more in line with the literary prop of storytellers implying veracity for their fictional character or persona as a type of framing device, particularly when mixed with inclusion of true historical events and anecdotes; popular examples of this craft-technique could be compared alongside works such as *The Amityville Horror* by Jay Anson; *The Woman in Black: A Ghost Story* by Susan Hill; *Robinson Crusoe* by Daniel Defoe; and even the classic of horror epistolary fiction, *Dracula* by Bram Stoker.

In other words, simply because the author states, "This is a true story," does not prove it so.

Further supposition involves looking past *Indian Ghost Stories* to Mukerji's first work, *The Mysterious Traders*, which involves rapscallion Americans fleeing to England where they band together to rob the London gentry. At its heart, it is as "English" to Crime/Detective Fiction as one can get, sans bowler hat or smoking pipe. The tale is set firmly in the pantheon of Victorian/Edwardian (or "Romantic") era and sensibility aligning with other such works as *The Red Thumb Mark* by R. Austin Freeman or *The Mystery of a Hansom Cab* by Fergus Hume (not to mention the canon of Sherlock Holmes or of Edgar Allan Poe's tales of C. Auguste Dupin).

Why then publish that first work under a predominantly Bangladeshi surname?

I believe Mukerji did live in India. His publisher, after all, is in Allahabad rather than London. Perhaps the native-sounding *nom de plume* was to set his writing apart from scores of other British authors. Perhaps it was in homage to another Mukerji-inspired individual or event. Perhaps it was a work for hire, a marketing gimmick, or completely at the publisher's doing. Notably in *Indian Ghost Stories*, Mukerji does have knowledge of details of Indian culture and society that most outside the country probably would not be aware, although his writing also displays more of an "observational" tone of Indian life, rather than any depth of personal experience or struggle. All this to say that the matter does not detract from the quality and entertainment of these fabulous stories, but only to suggest perhaps an issue of presumed cultural appropriation.

Who was S.(N.) Mukerji truly? It would be satisfying to discover and ascertain the accuracy of my humble (and entirely indulgent) speculations. But by now the truth, unfortunately, may already be lost to fading, fleeting tomes, as like most of literary history.

—Eric J. Guignard
Chino Hills, California
July 21, 2024

Illustration by Ernest Griset from *Vikram and the Vampire, or Tales of Hindu Devilry* by Richard F. Burton, F.R.G.S. (1870).

SUGGESTED FURTHER READING OF RELATED FICTION

For readers who have enjoyed *The Collected Works of S. Mukerji*, the following is a small selection of excellent and commensurable English-language books of supernatural fiction set in India that are of similar voice, theme, or literary style.

Afterlife: Ghost Stories from Goa by Jessica Faleiro (2012): A collection of intertwined haunting short stories told by family members during a blackout in India's smallest state.

Betaal Panchabinsati (*Twenty-Five [Tales] of the Phantom*) by Ishwar Chandra Vidyasagar (1847): A collection of connected tales (translated from Sanskrit) regarding the attempted capture of a trickster spirit.

The Book of Indian Ghosts by Riksundar Banerjee (2021): A guide to the supernatural entities of India including legends, myths, ghosts, and folklore.

The Calcutta Chromosome by Amitav Ghosh (1995): A mysterious turn of events sends a computer programmer on a life-changing quest into the history of malaria, in this medical thriller that won the Arthur C. Clarke Award for best science fiction novel.

The Collected Short Stories by Satyajit Ray (2012): A collection of forty-nine short stories of the macabre and supernatural by this author who is also considered one of the most influential film directors of India.

Darkness by Ratnakar Matkari (translated from Marathi by Vikrant Pande) (2019): A collection of the best short horror stories by this renowned Indian author, columnist, and movie producer.

The Devourers by Indra Das (2015): Complex saga of a professor who must transcribe the unfished tales of a half-werewolf, exploring centuries of history through the lens of fantasy, mythology, and social taboos.

Folk-Tales of Bengal by Lal Behari Dey (1883): One of the most famous collections of folk and fairy tales from India, beautifully illustrated by Warwick Goble.

Ghost Stories from the Raj (an anthology) edited by Ruskin Bond (1985): An anthology of nineteen classic short ghost stories penned during British-colonial India.

Ghosts of the Silent Hills: Stories Based on True Hauntings by Anita Krishan (2019): A collection of haunting short stories based on local lore of India in both rural and urban settings.

Indian Detective Stories by S. B. Banerjea (Satya Bhushan Bandyopadhyay) (1911): A collection of short detective-thriller fiction stories solving crimes in India (by author of *The Adventures of Mrs. Russell* <1904>).

Indian Tales by Rudyard Kipling (1890): A collection of short stories set in British colonial India by one of the Victorian era's most popular authors.

Mad Sisters of Esi by Tashan Mehta (2023): A fantasy novel of Indian folklore and tragedy, set in the belly of a mythical whale.

The Mine by Arnab Ray (2011): Horror thriller with explicit gore of a haunted mine built atop an ancient place of worship.

Mosquito and Other Stories by Premendra Mitra (2004): A posthumous collection of twelve Ghana-da (*character*) tales mixing fantasy and science in "probable" situations.

Night Theater by Vikram Paralkar (2017): Debut novel about a rural doctor tasked to heal the wounds of a dead, talking family before sunrise.

The Other Side: Dare to Visit Alone? by Faraaz Kazi and Vivek Banerjee (2013): A collection of thirteen tales of the paranormal by this collaboration of Kazi (a romance author) and Banerjee (a horror film maker) with claim to have "the world's first animated book cover."

Penguin Book of Indian Ghost Stories (an anthology) edited by Ruskin Bond (1993): Another Ruskin Bond anthology of stories set in Colonial India, this with twenty-two tales (including the editor's own work).

Strength of Water by Jayaprakash Satyamurthy (2019): A slim novella in which a boy and a girl—both young college students—fantasize about trading places as a fascist regime comes to power in India.

Thakurmar Jhuli (an anthology) edited by Dakshinaranjan Mitra Majumder (as "Thakurmar Jhuli") (1907): An anthology of Bengali folk tales and fairy tales (now renowned as children's literature).

That Frequent Visitor by K. Hari Kumar (2015): A romantic horror novel of a haunted house and childhood memories that prove distorted.

"To Let" Etc. by B.M. (Bithia Mary) Croker (1893): A collection of eight tales of ghosts and haunted buildings that also explores themes of gender, class, and colonization.

Vikram and the Vampire, or Tales of Hindu Devilry by Richard F. Burton, F.R.G.S. (1870): A translation of eleven (of the twenty-five) Hindu fairy tales told by a Baital (a huge Bat, Vampire, or Evil Spirit which inhabits and animates dead bodies).

The Witch in the Peepul Tree by Arefa Tehsin (2023): A whodunit horror mystery set in the 1950s of north-western India, involving a dead teen boy and several complex and caste-conscious suspects.

Yakshini by Neil D'Silva (2019): A modern teen girl with a Yakshini (nature spirit) living unbeknownst inside her seeks revenge against those who have done her wrong in this mythology-based supernatural horror novel.

The Zamindar's Ghost by Khayaal Patel (2023): Thought dead, a Zamindar (type of feudal landowner) returns home in 1933, only to face mysterious deaths, deceptions, and government turmoil in this horror-suspense novel.

Uncredited lithograph of Ganesha, god of wisdom,
success, and good luck. (ca. 1878–1883).

EDITOR'S REQUEST

DEAR reader, fan, or supporter,

It's a dreadful commentary that the worth of indie publications is measured by online 5-star reviews, but such is the state of current commerce.

Should you have enjoyed this book, gratitude is most appreciated by posting a brief and honest online review at Amazon.com, Goodreads.com, and/or a highly-visible blog.

With sincerest thanks,

Eric J. Guignard
Editor, *The Collected Works of S. Mukerji:*
Indian Ghost Stories and The Mysterious Traders

ALSO FROM ERIC J. GUIGNARD AND DARK MOON BOOKS:

Death. Who has not considered their own mortality and wondered at what awaits, once our frail human shell expires? What occurs after the heart stops beating, after the last breath is drawn, after life as we know it terminates?

Does our spirit remain on Earth while the body rots? Do the remnants of our soul transcend to a celestial Heaven or sink to Hell's torment? Can we choose our own afterlife? Can we die again in the hereafter? Are we given the opportunity to reincarnate and do it all over? Is life merely a cosmic joke or is it an experiment for something greater? Enclosed in this Bram Stoker-award winning anthology are thirty-four all-new dark and speculative fiction stories exploring the possibilities *AFTER DEATH* . . .

Illustrated by Audra Phillips and including stories by: Steve Rasnic Tem, Bentley Little, John Langan, Lisa Morton, and exceptional others.

"Though the majority of the pieces come from the darker side of the genre, a solid minority are playful, clever, or full of wonder. This strong anthology is sure to make readers contemplative even while it creates nightmares."

—*Publishers Weekly*

"In Eric J. Guignard's latest anthology he gathers some of the biggest and most talented authors on the planet to give us their take on this entertaining and perplexing subject matter . . . highly recommended."

—*Famous Monsters of Filmland*

"An excellent collection of imaginative tales of what waits beyond the veil."

—*Amazing Stories Magazine*

Order your copy at www.darkmoonbooks.com or www.amazon.com
ISBN-13: 978-0-9885569-2-8

THE CRIME FILES OF KATY GREEN by GENE O'NEILL:

Discover why readers have been applauding this stark, fast-paced noir series by multiple-award-winning author, Gene O'Neill, and follow the dark murder mysteries of Sacramento homicide detectives Katy Green and Johnny Cato, dubbed by the press as Sacramento's "Green Hornet and Cato"!

Book #1: *DOUBLE JACK* (a novella)

400-pound serial killer Jack Malenko has discovered the perfect cover: He dresses as a CalTrans worker and preys on female motorists in distress in full sight of passing traffic. How fast can Katy Green and Johnny Cato track him down before he strikes again?

ISBN-13: 978-0-9988275-6-8

Book #2: *SHADOW OF THE DARK ANGEL*

Bullied misfit, Samuel Kubiak, is visited by a dark guardian angel who helps Samuel gain just vengeance. There hasn't been a case yet Katy and Johnny haven't solved, but now how can they track a psychopathic suspect that comes and goes in the shadows?

ISBN-13: 978-0-9988275-8-2

Book #3: *DEATHFLASH*

Billy Williams can see the soul as it departs the body, and is "commanded to do the Lord's work," which he does fanatically, slaying drug addicts in San Francisco…Katy and Johnny investigate the case as junkies die all around, for Billy has his own addiction: the rush of viewing the *Deathflash*.

ISBN-13: 978-0-9988275-9-9

Order your copy at www.darkmoonbooks.com or www.amazon.com

ABOUT THIS BOOK'S EDITOR

ERIC J. GUIGNARD is a writer and editor of dark and speculative fiction, operating from the shadowy outskirts of Los Angeles, where he also runs the small press Dark Moon Books. He's twice won the Bram Stoker Award (the highest literary award of horror fiction), won the Shirley Jackson Award, and been a finalist for the World Fantasy Award and International Thriller Writers Award.

He has over one hundred stories and non-fiction author credits appearing in publications around the world. As editor, Eric's published multiple fiction anthologies, including his most recent, *Professor Charlatan Bardot's Travel Anthology to the Most (Fictional) Haunted Buildings in the Weird, Wild World* and *A World of Horror*, each a showcase of international horror short fiction. His next anthology is a Middle Grade-revisiting of classic literature tales, *Scaring and Daring*, to be released 2025 by HarperCollins.

He currently publishes the acclaimed series of author primers created to champion modern masters of the dark and macabre, *Exploring Dark Short Fiction*. He is also publisher and acquisitions editor for the renowned *+Horror Library+* anthology series. Formerly, he was curator of the series, *Haunted Library of Horror Classics*, through SourceBooks with co-editor Leslie S. Klinger.

His latest books are *Last Case at a Baggage Auction*; *Doorways To The Deadeye*; and short story collection *That Which Grows Wild: 16 Tales of Dark Fiction* (Cemetery Dance). His second collection, *A Graveside Gallery: Tales of Ghosts and Dark Matters*, will be out 2025 (Cemetery Dance) and forthcoming is his next novel, *Wrecked, Yet Sent Forth*.

Outside the glamorous and jet-setting world of indie fiction, Eric's a technical writer and college professor, and he stumbles home each day to a wife, children, dogs, and a terrarium filled with mischievous beetles. Visit Eric at: www.ericjguignard.com; Twitter: @ericjguignard; or his blog: ericjguignard.blogspot.com.

Interior illustration by W. (Warwick) Goble from *Folk-tales of Bengal* (1912).
Herein, a score of demons erupt from a Brahman's vessel.

9 781949 491579